CHRISTMAS CAT BLUES

THE CLEVER CAT MYSTERIES
BOOK 5

ALISON O'LEARY

For Sharon

1

────────

AUBREY SETTLED MORE COMFORTABLY on the roof of Molly's car as he watched the delivery man wrangle a large tree from the back of the open truck and drag it up to the front door, clutching it around the trunk and pulling it behind him. Next to him, Vincent continued the slow languid washing of his right ear. Leaning back against the porch, the man closed his eyes for a moment and drew a deep breath before making his way back to the truck. Jumping down from the car, Aubrey padded over to the porch. He could smell the tree already, a fragrant resiny smell that scented the cold winter air. He raised his head and looked up into the slate grey sky. Snow was on the way.

────────

INSIDE FIRESIDE HOUSE, a pair of cold eyes followed the visitor as he made his way around the large open plan office, hand extended to the women who had instinctively risen from their chairs on his entrance as if he was some sort of visiting royalty. He was good-looking though, he had to admit it. Tall and handsome in that old-fashioned movie star way, with a square chin and bright blue eyes that crinkled around the corners in a way that suggested he had a ready smile. His fair hair flopped very slightly over his forehead and gave an almost boyish charm to his appearance. The sharp cut of his grey suit, the crisp blue shirt and the designer tie added to the effect, too. But be that as it may, this bloke was going to make enemies if he kept poking his nose into the workings of the Foundation, that was for sure.

He continued watching as the man stopped to talk to Lucy, leaning over and looking interested in what she was working on. Lucy, sucking in her stomach, fluttered her eyelashes at him as she showed him some of the case files. He narrowed his eyes. This new chairman of trustees was nothing like the previous chairman, Charles. In fact, Charles, with his fat belly pushing against his shirt buttons and his propensity to start sweating after two glasses of wine had been almost the complete opposite. It would never have occurred to Charles to show any more interest in the office staff than he would have done in a new printer. As far as Charles was concerned, the staff were just a part of the fabric of the building. He had certainly never bothered to speak to any of them. He doubted that Charles had even known their names. The only times that Charles was seen around Fireside House was when he had attended the quarterly meeting of the trustees, meetings at which he'd thrown his not inconsiderable weight around. He had been fond of Charles though, in a lukewarm sort of way. He had certain qualities. The main one being his complete disinterest in the affairs of The Family Fireside Foundation, other than the opportunity it gave him to be king of the castle for the day.

Outside the snow began to fall, the soft white flakes swirling and brushing against the windows. In the distance, the sound of the waves crashing against the sea wall could just be heard.

2

___

CARLOS LAY on his stomach on the rug in front of the fire, flicking the pages of a football magazine. He looked up as Jeremy came in, followed by Vincent who slipped in behind him and joined Aubrey under the Christmas tree which was waiting to be decorated.

"Snowed off," said Jeremy. "Where's Molly?"

"Here," said Molly, coming through from the kitchen. "Did you have something to eat at the golf club?"

Jeremy shook his head.

"No, I had a quick drink with some of the lads and then came straight back in case the weather got worse. I had a chat with one of the new members, Adam something or other. Interesting bloke. He struck me as being one of those eager types, but not in a painful way, if you know what I mean. Not like Ernest." He laughed. "Ernest by name, earnest by nature. God, who calls their child Ernest these days? Although it's probably popular again now, like Albert and Enid."

"Is Ernest still teaching at Sir Frank's?" asked Molly.

"Last I heard. Amazing when you think about it. The smart

money in the staff room was on him making a bolt for it before the end of his first term."

"You have to give him credit for sticking with it," said Molly, sitting down in the chair next to the fire. "Even after the ankle biting incident. What was it he used to say?"

Jeremy assumed a sombre expression and sank his chin slightly into his chest.

"All children are a gift and we must treat them accordingly. He didn't mention unwanted gifts. But he had a kind of air of innocence about him that you couldn't help liking. I can seem him now, huddled outside in a cloud of tobacco smoke, even when it was raining. He never did what the other smokers on the staff used to do."

"Why, what did they do?"

"Head off to the big cupboard in the art room. They chucked all the art stuff out and made it into a sort of little club room. They had chairs and a rug in there and everything."

"Didn't the art teacher mind?"

"It was his idea. I suppose," he continued, "it was a sort of alternative staff room."

"Didn't the head object?"

"She pretended that she didn't know. Otherwise she might have had to do something about it. Anyway, amongst his other worthy contributions to the well-being of life at Sir Frank's, Ernest used to run the fund-raising events and ask the kids for ideas. Honestly, you should have seen some of the suggestions."

Carlos looked up again from his magazine and grinned.

"Yeah, I remember those. The best one was the annual granny fight."

"The what?" asked Molly.

"Annual granny fight. It was Frankie Gibbon's idea. He said that we should round up all the grannies in the neighbourhood and have a big bundle in the playground at the end of the summer term and we could charge for tickets and take bets."

"Yes, well," said Jeremy. "Frankie Gibbons had a vested interest. His granny weighed about forty stone and could have given Mike Tyson a run for his money." He shuddered slightly. "I still have nightmares about the time she turned up at parents evening instead of Frankie's mother. It was practically a medical phenomenon."

"What was?" Molly looked perplexed.

"The development of simultaneous spontaneous migraine which necessitated some staff having to exit rapidly."

Molly laughed.

"What did Ernest say about the suggestion for a granny fight?"

"Well, of course he took it very seriously and said that he'd look into it but the school might have difficulty arranging insurance. Honestly, he just couldn't see that the kids were taking the piss out of him half the time. Mind you, when he was rushed to hospital with appendicitis they did have a whip round and take him in sixty Benson and Hedges and a potted chrysanthemum."

Molly leaned forward and tickled Vincent under the chin, who stretched his paws in front of him and inched a little closer to her. Aubrey smiled. When Vincent had first joined the household he had hung back as though afraid to get too close to them. Now he looked forward to their coming home as much as Aubrey did.

"So, tell me about this Adam," said Molly. "Presumably he's local?"

Jeremy nodded.

"Moved here about two months ago. One of those big houses up on the headland, the ones with the huge bay windows. He's the southern area manager of one of the big banks. I can't remember which one now, although he did say.

He's also just been appointed as the Chair of trustees for the Family Fireside Foundation."

"Has he?" Molly looked interested. "That's where we donated some of the funds from our last social event at the Lodge. It was quite a lot in the end. The residents really threw themselves into it, it was great fun. Mind you, at the time it was just what everybody needed. It was just after…"

Aubrey yawned and tucked his tail more tightly around himself. He remembered the social event well. It had been arranged not long after the murder at the Lilac Tree Lodge care home for the elderly and both he and Vincent, as participants in the visiting pets scheme, had been allowed to go. They had spent most of the day observing the elderly residents and their visitors playing hoop-la and running egg and spoon races on the lawns, although the latter had ended in some disarray after two of the residents started brawling and hurling eggs at each other after one of them accused the other of deliberately tripping him. As Molly said, it was a good job that the eggs were hard-boiled. He had even submitted to the indignity of the 'guess the weight of the cat' competition although he had been less impressed when some bright spark had written 'five tons' on the entry slip. He didn't know how much five tons was but it seemed like a lot.

"I've heard that the Foundation do a lot of good work with the homeless," continued Molly. "Which is why we donated some of our funds to it. I hadn't realised until we moved here what a problem homelessness can be in coastal areas. I suppose that I'd always associated being homeless with inner cities."

Jeremy nodded.

"Adam was telling me about it. Part of the problem is that employment tends to be seasonal which obviously causes problems in the winter months, and also these areas seem to attract drifters. I can't say I blame them. I suppose if you've got nothing, you might as well have nothing in nice surroundings. And then there's the drug scene, although you get that everywhere."

"I guess so," said Molly. "So what does the Foundation do in practical terms?"

"Quite a lot, one way and another. One of the things that they do is buy up old properties and convert them into flats. And they acquire land and build new blocks sometimes as well. One of their policies is to try to re-home people with a drugs problem away from the area. To give them a fresh start."

"How do they decide who to give homes to? Do people just apply?"

"I think that they can, but it's mostly done through referrals. Like social services or other charities."

"Where do they get their money from?" asked Molly. "It can't all be fund-raising."

"I think that the fund-raising is mostly for public relations purposes, it helps them attract legacies. But they have a portfolio of investments that they finance most of the work with, as well as a substantial amount in a trust fund. And of course, they do get rents from the properties."

Carlos put his magazine aside.

"The original foundation was started by Sir George Renton. When he was a boy, his father died when he was seven and left his mother with six children and no money. They lived rough for a while in the caves on the beach and he said that it was an experience that he never forgot. After he got rich, he set up the Family Fireside Foundation to help families in difficulties but now they help single people as well."

Molly looked at Carlos in astonishment.

"How on earth do you know all that?"

"There was a piece in the local paper."

Jeremy smiled slightly. Carlos taking an interest in current affairs, even if only at a local level, was a new development. He was definitely maturing.

"How did Sir George make his money?" asked Molly

"Buttons and stuff. Like, making them. Which," Carlos added thoughtfully, "was dead clever when you think about it. I mean, like, everything has buttons. Even nowadays. I bet there's, like, millions of buttons even in just this house."

Molly thought for a moment and then nodded. Carlos was right. There were probably at least a dozen buttons on the clothes that they were wearing now. She turned to Jeremy.

"How does the Foundation work then? I mean, who actually runs it now?"

"It's run like any other business really. It's just that their business is charitable. A group of trustees make the decisions on policy and planning and so on and then there are paid staff who put it into practice. A bit like the government and the Civil Service, I suppose. The Foundation's got a Chief Executive plus proper managers to handle things like finance and human resources as well as a fund raising and public relations department. Like I said, just like any other business."

"Right." Molly nodded. "So are the trustees volunteers? I mean, they're not paid or anything?"

"Only expenses," said Jeremy. "Funnily enough, Adam was telling me that there's a vacancy on the board and they're looking for someone who lives locally. He asked me if I would consider him putting my name forward."

"And will you?"

"Probably. I think it might be interesting. Something different, anyway."

3

______

MOLLY PEERED into the cardboard box and pulled out a fat wax candle in the shape of Father Christmas. She tipped her head to one side and regarded it fondly.

"Goodness. We've had this for years. Since our first Christmas together, I think."

"So a genuine antique then?" said Carlos. "You ought to take it on the Road Show. It could be worth a fortune. I'll check for the next time it's coming to town."

Molly made a pretend swipe towards his head.

"Cheeky. Make yourself useful and unravel the fairy lights."

She delved into the box again and threw a great tangle of wires towards him. Despite their promises to themselves each year to make sure that the lights were properly stored, every year they got thrown in the box with the rest of the decorations with the result that every year they had to be untangled. From their observation post beneath the Christmas tree, Aubrey and Vincent watched with interest as Carlos shook the tangle down before starting to pick it apart, his long thin fingers delicately separating the strings. Aubrey always liked it when the Christmas decorations came out. It put everyone in a good mood and it was only a matter of time before the big turkey got cooked which always resulted in plenty of leftovers for him. If he could resist jumping up at the tree that is. Last year he had been marched from the house in disgrace after making a flying sideways leap at a spectacularly tantalising bauble and bringing the whole lot crashing down. It had taken quite a long time of pushing his face against the window and looking pathetic before they relented and let him back in again.

"What time do you think Jeremy will be back?" asked Carlos, an expression of fierce concentration on his face as he bent over the fairy lights.

Molly glanced at her watch.

"Anytime now I should think."

"So if he does this trustee thing, what does he have to do? Is it just, like, meetings and that?"

"I'm not sure to be honest," Molly admitted. "He'll tell us when he comes in. Talk of the devil," she added as the front door banged.

"Evening all," said Jeremy, pushing open the door. "This all looks very festive."

He sank down on the sofa and reached towards the bottle of wine and glasses that stood on the coffee table.

"So how did it go?" asked Molly, shaking a rope of tinsel stars from the box.

"Fine. Interesting." He poured himself a glass of wine and sat back. "We went to The Fox where Adam told me about some of the other trustees. "From the sound of it, there seem to be quite a few of the big-bellied self-important brigade and most of them close to retirement. I think that, apart from Adam, I would probably be the youngest by about ten or fifteen years."

"No women?"

Jeremy shook his head.

"No. Adam said that the previous chairman, Charles something, was a bit of a misogynist and the rest of the board followed suit. Charles was of the opinion that the only place for women at the Foundation was doing the office work and making the tea. None of the senior managers are women. Adam said that once he's got his feet under the table, he's going to make a real effort to appoint some women to the board. The problem is having to wait until somebody retires or resigns and then getting the others to agree. In the meantime, he's going to look at staffing and see if anything can be done there. Some training or promotion or something. Apparently, the office staff haven't even got proper job titles. Adam said that everybody just calls them 'the girls', even though a number of them are middle-aged."

"So how did Adam get appointed?"

"Usual story. The old boys' network. Adam's manager was about to retire, he's an old school friend of Charles. They've kept in touch over the years and Charles happened to mention that he was also retiring and that they were looking for somebody to replace him at the Foundation. Deal done. To be fair, I guess that was sort of how I was recruited, too.

"Didn't one of the existing trustees want to take over?" asked Molly.

Jeremy grinned.

"According to Adam, volunteers for the role were particularly conspicuous by their absence. He thinks that it's because they're frightened that they might have to do something other than turn up for meetings on expenses. Charles did little enough and I suspect that the other trustees do even less. In theory, the trustees propose policy but in reality I think that they more or less rubber stamp anything that's put in front of them. I can see why Adam wants to change things. It sounds like it was running a bit like a Victorian gentlemen's club."

Molly nodded.

"Did he explain what the role of trustee involves? What it should involve, I mean."

Jeremy nodded.

"Pretty much. He told me how the trust works. What I'd have to do and so on. It sounds really interesting."

Carlos crawled over to the light socket and plugged in the fairy lights. He sat back on his heels, head to one side, and smiled.

"Excelente!" He turned back to look at Jeremy. "Do you have to do it in your own time or will you get time off work?"

"Well, obviously I'll have to get approval from the Inspectorate but they're generally pretty good when people are volunteering. And, given that I work a lot from home now, it would probably just mean juggling things around a bit. There's four meetings a year plus a special trustees' meeting so I can't see it making too much impact on the inspection work."

Molly nodded. Jeremy's work as one of Her Majesty's Inspector of Schools was very important to him, she knew. Sometimes, she thought, too important. It would be good for him to have another interest.

"Actually," he continued, "Adam has invited me to sit in on one of their meetings and also asked me to their trustees annual Christmas lunch, even though I don't take my place on the board until the new year."

"Where's it held?" asked Molly.

"At a local hotel. All the staff at the Foundation and the trustees get together and have a three course meal paid for by the Foundation. The highlight apparently is the chairman's speech, followed by the chairman's toast. They have a claret jug that they bring out every year, one of those glass things with a silver top. It belonged to Sir George Renton, and the chairman pours from it and raises the toast. They're really careful with it. It's only used by the Chairman for the toast and then it goes back into wraps. To be honest, it all sounds a bit boring."

4

MAX SWEPT the snow from the windscreen of his car with the back of his gloved hand and glanced across to the road outside. If the traffic continued at this snail's pace it would be past midnight before he got home. He felt a twitch of irritation. Anybody would think that the country had never seen snow before. He got in the car and switched on the radio. The sound of Hark The Herald Angels boomed back at him. He switched it off and hunched his shoulders, glancing up at the windows of Fireside House. A large stripey creature with a white tip to his bib, paws and feet stared implacably back at him, its tail wrapped tightly around its body. He felt a spurt of anger. Eric. He hated that bloody animal. Every night when he left the building he made a point of finding it and chucking it out. And every morning it was back inside. How it had come to be living in Fireside House, nobody seemed to know. It had just turned up one day. And of course, the office staff loved it. Once they started feeding it, that was it. They were stuck with the creature. He wouldn't mind if it did anything useful like catch a few mice but all it seemed to do was sleep and wind him up.

He tipped his head back against the head rest and let his mind drift back over the day. He had been as startled as the next one when the new chairman had turned up unexpectedly. They should have been given some warning that he was coming. He shouldn't be allowed to just drop in when he felt like it. He felt a sudden frill of panic, an unexpected sensation that he'd been experiencing on and off all afternoon. The last thing that any of them needed was for somebody to start being overly interested in the affairs of the Foundation. It had unsettled the office staff too, so much so that they had more or less wasted most of the afternoon until one of them had suggested putting up the Christmas decorations and started dragging out the plastic cartons stored in the office cupboard. They had already begun the annual grimfest known as the Secret Santa days ago and it was seriously getting on his nerves. Whatever sadist invented it ought to be shot. Or better still, lashed to a holly tree and pelted with plum puddings. Preferably rock hard ones.

The maximum spend agreed by the staff was a fiver. A mingy fiver. It was a joke. Honestly, what could you buy for a fiver? Nothing that anybody would actually want, that was for sure. The result was that everybody ended up with stupid jokey presents that almost certainly went in the bin as soon as they got home. Last year he had received a pair of red socks which rang out Jingle Bells every time he moved. But he'd got his revenge this year. He had bought Sue, whose name he had picked out of the hat, some cheap bath foam. That'd get her eczema itching.

He huddled further into himself while he thought about the office staff. They were all right, he supposed. He'd worked with worse. At least they didn't go around treading on each other's heads to get promotion. Mostly on the basis that there was no promotion available to get, no matter how hard they worked. There was only one job title available in the general office and that was 'clerical and administration'. By virtue of age and experience, one or two of the women were considered to be more senior and supervised younger members of staff but there was no official recognition of that. But by and large, lack of career opportunities notwithstanding, they did a good job of coping with the day to day affairs of the Foundation. There were very few problems that they couldn't deal with, even those that came in the form of potential clients turning up unannounced at Fireside House. Those that did were usually in a state of agitation and, sometimes, inebriation, but one of the women would make him or her a cup of tea and start ringing around the relevant agencies to get some immediate relief.

If he was honest, he had to admit to himself that several of the women would have made good senior managers. Not that they would ever have the chance under the regime that the Chief Executive maintained. The Chief Executive's idea of rewarding the office staff topped out at giving them an afternoon off to do their Christmas shopping. This was on the basis that, at Christmas, the women did all the food and present shopping as well as all the cooking on the day, while the men toasted their arses in front of the fire and smoked cigars. But even that little bonus wasn't guaranteed. The women had to wait until he announced it, which he did by striding into the general office and announcing magnanimously that the office would be closing at lunchtime. And then, of course, they all had to thank him.

Making himself a cup of tea in the small kitchen that afternoon and reluctant to go back to his office, Max had deliberately taken his time while he watched them decorate the office and talk about Adam and what to wear to the annual Christmas lunch. Like it was Royal Ascot or something, he thought. It was only a meal at a hotel. It wasn't even a very good meal. Last year there had been insufficient potatoes and the Christmas pudding and brandy sauce had been unpleasantly tepid. The best bit had been when Charles had argued with one of the waiters over a bottle of wine, which Charles had claimed was corked. As if he could tell. He was just showing off in front of the office workers, most of whom had done their best to look suitably impressed while probably thinking what a twat he was. And the speeches were appalling, with everyone wearing their happy smiles plastered all over their faces and pretending to be interested. And as for the chairman's toast… although, this year it was a new chairman which would at least make a change from Charles trying to read his notes and dropping his glasses.

His expression soured still further as he thought about the trustees. Ten of them in total and what did they actually do? Turned up a few times a year to pontificate at meetings on subjects about which they knew nothing and cared even less, and staying at five star hotels for the privilege. He half suspected some of them of deliberately taking longer travel routes so that they could bump up their mileage claims. Then, after lording it about for a few hours, they went back to their tedious little lives and looked forward to the next time they could turn up at Fireside House and think themselves important. He sighed and leaned forward, reaching for the key to start the engine. He might as well make a move, he'd be sitting here all night otherwise.

———

THE DOWNSTAIRS WAS in darkness as he drew up, just a faint light showing in the front bedroom window. She'd obviously taken herself off to bed. Good. That meant with a bit of luck he wouldn't have to see her before the morning. It wouldn't have killed her to put the outside lights on though. He parked the car and let himself in, trying not to make a sound. Too late. The landing light snapped on. He looked up the stair well to the cross face of his step-mother staring down at him, the grubby pink quilted dressing gown falling open to reveal a stained nightdress.

"About bloody time. I've been waiting hours for you. I had to get my own supper."

He suppressed a sigh. It had seemed such a good idea at the time. After his father had died and left the house to both of them their first thought had been to sell it and split the proceeds. But the more they had thought about it, the more it seemed to make sense to keep it. It was a big detached four-bedroomed house with plenty of space for both of them. They had always got on pretty well and Stella had still been working then. He'd sold his own little house on the new estate and moved in. With a little effort and their own sitting rooms and bathrooms they had hardly seen each other. But since she had retired she had sunk further and further into herself and now he seemed to have found himself in the role of reluctant carer.

He looked up again into the sour wrinkled face. For God's sake, the woman could at least brush her hair instead of letting it hang down in lank strands and when was the last time she had seen a dentist? Stella had been a smart woman when his father had first met her, an office manager with a trim figure and a wide smile. He wouldn't recognise her now. In just ten short years she had gone from being an attractive woman in late middle-age to a shrivelled old shrew with bad breath.

He turned his back on her and went through to the kitchen. Shutting the door firmly behind him he poured himself a beer and leaned back against the work surface. If only the old cow would take a tumble down the stairs.

5

CARLOS PULLED the carrot out of his parka pocket and poked it into the large lump of snow and then carefully placed two pieces of coal above it. Pulling his scarf in the colours of the Brazilian national football team from his neck he tied it with a flourish around the place where the two boulders of snow met. From the warmth and safety of the kitchen window sill, paws tucked neatly beneath them, Aubrey and Vincent watched as he stood back and admired his handiwork. Aubrey turned to Vincent.

"What is it?"

"A snowman."

"A what?"

"A snowman. A man made out of snow."

Aubrey tipped his head to one side and looked again at the big white lop-sided figure.

"What's it for?"

Vincent shrugged.

"Dunno mate."

They both turned at the sound of a car driving slowly along the road, the driver sticking in second gear and inching along to avoid skidding. They watched as Jeremy got out and pulled his coat more tightly around him. Spotting them on the window sill he grinned and waved and then, sighting Carlos he bent down and gathered a handful of snow. Patting it carefully into a ball, he took aim and struck Carlos squarely on the back. Carlos spun round and immediately gathered up a great ball of snow of his own and lobbed it in Jeremy's direction, running for cover to the far corner of the garden as he did so. Aubrey and Vincent watched in amazement, their heads flicking from side to side as the snow balls came thick and fast until, at last, Jeremy put his hands up in breathless surrender.

"What on earth…?" Molly leaned forward and peered out of the window. "They'll be soaked."

She turned as the back door opened and Jeremy came in, stamping the snow from his shoes and rubbing his hands together, his eyes bright and his hair damp. Behind him crept Carlos, hand raised with one final snowball.

"Carlos…" warned Molly.

He pulled a face and threw the snowball back outside.

Molly smiled, a warm indulgent smile that belied the harshness of her warning.

"I'll stick the kettle on," she said. "So," turning to Jeremy, "how did it go? Was it interesting?"

"Funnily enough," he said, "It was. You know, I must have passed Fireside House dozens of times but I've never really noticed it before. And yet it's in the middle of the high street."

"Is it that big place, near to the department store? The one with the gates?" asked Carlos. "I go past there on my way to college."

Jeremy nodded.

"That's the one. It's weird. You go in and it's like a different world. You'd think that you were on a country estate or something. One minute you're on the busy high street and the next you're in this sort of peaceful parkland."

"Like Buckingham Palace," said Carlos.

Jeremy looked confused.

"What?"

"Buckingham Palace," repeated Carlos. "It's that house where the Queen lives."

Jeremy's mouth twitched.

"Yes, Carlos. I know where the Queen lives."

"Well, it's like the Queen and all the Dukes and that live in there, and outside it's London and loads of traffic and tourists and that."

Jeremy smiled.

"Well, Fireside House isn't quite like Buckingham Palace, but I know what you mean. Anyway," he continued, "there's parking round the back that leads out to the main road, and the grounds are just beautiful. Really well-looked after, they must have a gardener. And the house has been divided into offices but they've kept a lot of the original features so you can see what it was like when Sir George Renton lived there with his family. All the senior managers and the Chief Executive have their offices on the first floor and the admin staff have their office on the ground floor. The meeting was in the board room on the ground floor, too. I think that it must have been a formal dining room originally, it's got beautiful French doors that lead out into the grounds and a huge mahogany table and portraits on the wall."

"It sounds lovely," said Molly.

"It is. It's like stepping back into the past. It's not just the house. Everything seems to be run on old-fashioned lines. They've even got a tea lady who comes in every morning and afternoon and wheels a tea trolley round."

"Goodness," said Molly. "I thought that tea ladies were an extinct species."

"So did I," said Jeremy. "She's called Annie and apparently she's a bit of a character. The house has got a basement, too.

Adam showed it to me. All the old records are kept in it, dating right back to the nineteenth century, but most of the staff don't like going down there."

Carlos looked interested.

"Why? Is it haunted?"

Jeremy shook his head.

"No, I don't think so. It's just dark and dusty. It's one of the office rules that if anyone has to go down there to fetch anything, they have to tell someone where they're going in case they accidentally get locked in. It's got one of those heavy doors that swings shut automatically. It's usually propped open with a fire extinguisher but they ought to change it really. If you got stuck down there you could shout for hours and nobody would hear you."

Molly shuddered and handed Carlos and Jeremy a mug of hot chocolate each.

"Come on into the sitting room and dry off, the pair of you. The fire's lit."

Molly and Jeremy settled back on the sofa while Carlos took up his usual place on the rug, legs crossed and fingers wrapped around his mug. In the window bay the tiny lights on the Christmas tree twinkled in the firelight. Jeremy dipped his head and took a deep draught. He thought for a moment.

"It's funny. I didn't realise before how much I missed working with other people."

"But you work with other people now, don't you?" said Molly.

"Yes, I do, but it's not the same. A lot of it is working from home and you're not always on the same inspection team. You don't get the same interaction."

"What about when you go into schools? You're mixing with other people then, aren't you?"

"Not really. The thing is, from the time you step across the threshold, you're being observed. Everybody's watching you.

Everything that you say or do is noticed. And I understand that. It was the same at Sir Frank's. Whenever we had an inspection everybody was on high alert. Because it's all very well for people to say it doesn't matter, it's only an inspection, or whatever, because it does matter. A good inspection report can be the making of a school. And vice versa."

"But surely you talk to the staff and so on when you're there?"

"Yes, but they're not like colleagues that you see every day. Every conversation is very controlled. Quite often they've got prepared answers ready. We used to do it at Sir Frank's, too." He sighed and Molly looked at him, concerned. It was a good job that he'd have a break over Christmas, he sounded as if he needed it.

"I think," Jeremy continued, "that in some schools the staff think that we've just landed from Mars. They seem to forget that nearly all of us were serving teachers. Like I said, you're on show the whole time. I suppose that I've more or less got used to it now but well... I guess that being in that board room today made me feel more like a part of something. A member of a team. I couldn't actually join in yet of course, not officially. But it was good to see how it worked."

"So who was there?"

"Well, the Chief Executive and the senior managers, as well as the trustees. The Chief Executive, Dick, seems a bit useless. He was practically nodding off at one point. Adam told me that he's another one due to retire in the not too distant future. From the look of him, he's just counting down the days." He laughed suddenly. "Just after we got started, somebody had left the door ajar and a little cat drifted in and made itself at home on top of a side table. I swear it was listening to everything we said."

Aubrey and Vincent looked at each other. They had met Eric on their nightly rounds, which had lately included the bottom end of the high street and Fireside House. He had promised to show them the secret way in and give them a tour. They had a lot of respect for Eric. He didn't say much but he did a lot of thinking.

"Anyway," Jeremy continued. "Adam stirred things up a bit."

Molly leaned forward.

"Why? What did he do?"

"He started asking questions. Something to do with some project in the midlands. The Foundation is converting some big houses into flats. He asked how it was going, what the state of play is and so on. Everyone looked a bit surprised. I understand that the usual thing is for each senior manager to give an update and then they discuss it a bit and then it's more or less signed it off. Adam said that it might be useful to look at some of the stats and figures at some point. None of the managers looked very pleased."

"Did anybody actually object?"

"No, not exactly, but there was a sort of atmosphere if you know what I mean."

Carlos drained his mug and got to his feet.

"I think I'll go for a walk."

Jeremy watched him leave the room, his expression thoughtful.

"Is he all right? Apart from trying to murder me by snowball, he seems very quiet."

Molly gave a half-smile.

"He had an email from Teddy today."

———

DOWN ON THE beach Carlos wrapped his parka more tightly around him, feeling the cold wind bite into his face. He was regretting tying his scarf around the snowman now. He'd swap it for something else when he got back. He shouldn't leave it out anyway, it was one of the last reminders of his life in Brazil and he would be devastated if anything happened to it. He supposed that he could always get another scarf but it wouldn't be the same. His grandfather had given him that scarf when he was four and he had taken it everywhere with him ever since. He sat down on one of the big boulders that were strewn along the beach and stared out to sea.

Teddy was going away when she finished her A levels. She was going on this gap year thing, working in some orphanage or something. It had taken all his self-control not to plead with her not to go, to point out that he was an orphan too. His mother had been murdered and his father was almost certainly dead from the effects of alcoholism. He loved Molly and Jeremy dearly but they were his foster parents, not his real parents even though he pretended that they were sometimes. If Teddy went off to this orphanage place she would forget all about him. There were bound to be boys there. Posh boys with thick floppy hair and big perfect teeth and then she would probably go off and marry one of them and live in one of those big houses, the sort in which his mother had been employed as a cleaner. And then it would be all over. All his plans for finishing his catering course at college and starting a restaurant would mean nothing without her. He'd be finished before he got started. He dipped his head as he felt the hot pricking of tears against his eyelids.

6

———————

MAX STARED out of the window at the snow which was now falling fast, great fat flakes swirling in delicate fluffy formations before they finally settled. It showed no sign of slowing down and traffic was bound to be disrupted again. Really they all ought to go home early but it would never occur to Dick. He was far too selfish. Living within walking distance of Fireside House, the Chief Executive never considered that some people might occasionally have difficulties with travelling. Next to him Harry doodled on the agenda placed in front of him. They all hated these Monday management meetings. They were only for show anyway. Nothing was ever decided and even if it was, it was generally ignored. The truth was that they all went off and did their own thing. He picked up his pen and assumed an air of concentration as Dick started speaking. God, he was boring.

"And I know how very much we are all looking forward to the Christmas lunch this year…"

Max stared at him, his face impassive. He couldn't seriously believe that, could he? The annual farce where everybody pretended that they were all in it together? The trustees only turned out because it was a free lunch and a night in a decent hotel. It was pretty much the only time they ever saw any of the office staff. Most of them wouldn't have recognised one if she bit him on the bum. And in the case of some of the trustees there was a lot of bum to bite. Perhaps, though, Dick really did believe that the annual enforced jolliness was the social highlight of the year. He was stupid enough. He barely had one brain cell to crash against another. Only Dick could have introduced himself as Richard and then confidently invited his senior managers to 'call me Dick'. Which they did. How he had ever got this job in the first place was a complete mystery. Including, Max suspected, to Dick himself.

Dick continued.

"And the new brochures that Harry has produced are really quite magnificent. I think that we can all agree that the trustees were very pleased with them."

Harry glanced at the pile of brochures stacked on the end of the table. All in all, he had to agree with Dick, they were pretty nicely done. A class act. They'd look good in the reception area. The images were well-chosen, pathetic looking beneficiaries, but not too pathetic looking, nobody wanted to look at raddled druggies, and the quotes read well. All right, they hadn't exactly said what was printed in the brochure but that was what they meant. He had simply helped them to express themselves. He smiled to himself. He hadn't lied at the meeting of trustees when Adam had asked him if he had actually interviewed these people. He had interviewed them. Well, two of them, when he'd taken a trip out to the proposed new development outside Birmingham. It hadn't taken very long. The rest of the time he had spent getting to know his new girlfriend in the five star expenses paid hotel he'd booked. He looked around at his colleagues and waited in modest expectation for their praise.

"Very nice, Harry," said Nigel, economic as ever with words.

"Yes, I am rather pleased with them," Harry said, with his wide trademark smile that showed his perfectly straight and very expensive teeth, "And you'll be pleased to know that I managed to keep the costs down pretty well."

Max looked across at him and smiled back in spite of himself. Harry had all the charm that you'd expect of a man in his position. Responsible for fund-raising and public relations, Harry had thick dark hair with just a touch of silver at the temples, beautifully cut suits that screamed quality and a way of looking at somebody with an honest intensity as if they were the most important person in the world. The trustees loved him, the gullible idiots. But Harry's greatest quality was that he was a man who could keep his nerve under pressure. And right now, with the new Chairman taking an undue interest in the affairs of the Foundation, they needed that more than ever. He glanced across at Nigel. He was less sure of Nigel. As the IT and Finance manager, Nigel held a lot of power. He could make things appear and disappear at will. And he knew it. It wasn't helped by the fact that Nigel had even less to occupy himself during office hours than the rest of them. The post had only been created because at some point one of the trustees had said that all modern businesses had them. A small mole-like man with a habit of peering rather than looking at you, he sometimes had the sinking feeling that Nigel would shop the lot of them if it suited him.

"And Max," said Dick. "How is the new girl settling in? Finding her way around all right?"

"Fine, Dick. Absolutely fine."

Which was true. What wasn't absolutely fine was the persistence of the male applicant who had been better qualified and had more experience and was frankly a better candidate than Lettie, the teenaged girl that had been appointed. Lettie was a nice enough girl but she'd only just left school. Not surprisingly, the male candidate had wanted an explanation as to why he hadn't been offered the job. Max sighed inwardly. As Administrative manager with responsibility for human resources, he would have to deal with it somehow. He knew only too well that the appointment of a male would have gone down like the proverbial lead one with the trustees. Offices were for girls. They worked there until they got married and then they came back when their children started school. That was the way of the Fireside Foundation world and so far nobody had seen any reason to change it.

Dick swept his papers up.

"Must get on," he said, puffing his chest slightly. "Busy day. Some new legacies to look at."

The Chief Executive was the only staff member with any legal training although what the exact nature of that training had been was always rather vague and almost certainly so out of date to be of any real value. Nonetheless, it didn't stop him on occasion from giving the impression that the Lord Chancellor was regularly on the blower asking for advice. He paused as he reached the door, and turned back.

"Oh, by the way. Adam asked me for some background on the Foundation, he's keen to get to grips with the work that we do.. So I asked my secretary to give him some papers, minutes of meetings, newsletters, and so on to take away. I'm sure that I can rely on you chaps to give him any assistance that he requires."

The three managers smiled and nodded. They watched as he left the room, the tension among them suddenly rising. For a moment there was silence. Unseen by any of them, a striped cat sidled round the door and crept under a chair.

"Well?" said Max.

"Well what?" said Harry.

Nigel got up and quietly closed the door. He stood with his back to it and looked around him at his colleagues. Three more different men you probably couldn't hope to find, in both attitude and appearance. And yet the tie that held them was tighter than a hangman's noose.

7

———————

Max stared at Harry, his eyes narrowed.

"That's all we bloody need. God knows what Dick has given him. What are we going to do about it?"

"There's not much we can do, Max," said Harry. "Adam has been appointed as the Chairman of Trustees and that's that. Short of arranging for him to fall under a bus we're stuck with him. The best thing that we can do is keep our heads down and our mouths shut."

Nigel sat down again, put on his glasses, and drew in his breath.

"We all knew that it couldn't go on forever. We knew that it would have to end. It looks like it's going to have to be sooner rather than later, that's all."

Max turned to look at him, spitting out the words.

"Yes, well, that's not particularly helpful, is it Nigel? You were at the trustees meeting, you heard the questions he was asking. Christ," he pushed his hand through his hair. "I thought he was never going to shut up. And now he's got hold of God knows what paperwork."

Nigel opened his mouth to speak and then closed it again as Harry cut across him.

"All right, calm down." Harry's voice smoothed over the fractures that were threatening to erupt. "The next meeting of the trustees isn't until February. We've got plenty of time to think about things."

"There is the Christmas lunch though." Nigel spoke softly although there was nobody to hear him other than his colleagues and the cat that was watching him. Nigel's small brown eyes beetled over the top of his glasses as he waited for a response.

Harry sighed.

"Well, he's not going to start bringing up Foundation business over the lunch table is he? And if he does, we'll just have to change the subject somehow. It's supposed to be a social occasion, after all." He turned to Max. "What's the latest acquisition?"

"Hightrees Place."

"What did we pay for it?"

"£150K. The houses are practically derelict, they've been standing empty for years. They were up for demolition at some point but nobody ever got round to it."

Harry nodded.

"And what did the Foundation pay for it?"

"£450K."

"Ok. Well, we'd better make that the last one."

Max stood up and began walking around the room in long restless strides.

"We knew that we were safe under Charles, but this Adam is some sort of finance bloke. He works for a bank or something." He sat down again and began tapping on the table with the tips of his fingers as he spoke. "What if he starts looking into the company that the Foundation bought properties from? What if he does a search and finds out what the company paid for them?"

"Well, nobody has done so far. Anyway, why would he? The job of the trustees is to decide policy, not go poking around in admin."

"What if he goes to Companies House," Max persisted. "What if he puts two and two together?"

"Then he'll come up with nil, won't he Max? None of the registered directors can be traced to us." Harry looked suddenly doubtful. "Can they Nigel?"

Nigel shook his head. It had been his idea to use the identities of real people. More specifically, three specially chosen beneficiaries of the trust who were not only unknown to each other but were habitually so off their faces for most of the time that they barely knew what day of the week it was. He had access to all the files. He probably knew more about them than their own mothers. But whether or not they were addicts didn't matter. What mattered was that they existed. They had birth records, national insurance numbers, the lot. The registered office had been simple too. He had just used one of the registered office company address services.

"Very doubtful," he said. "Of course, in the unlikely event that the false entries are discovered, we'll all face prosecution for deliberately filling in false information on the register."

Harry laughed.

"Being prosecuted for offences under the Companies Act is going to be the least of our problems if this lot ever comes to light."

Nigel removed his glasses and began slowly polishing them. Typical Harry. Laugh it off. Breeze it all away. Well, he for one had no intention of being prosecuted for anything. He let his mind drift to the small laptop which sat in his study at home. He would challenge anyone, even the most forensically aware, to locate those files. He lifted his top lip in a slight smile. Sometimes he impressed even himself.

Harry looked at him suspiciously. What did Nigel have to smile about? He'd never really liked the man and he strongly suspected that the feeling was entirely mutual.

I think," Harry continued, speaking slowly, "the best thing to do is to make a strategic retreat. We knew it was going to have to come to an end when Dick retires anyway. We've had a good run. We can simply wind up the company. Let's get out while the going's good. But in the meantime we must stick together. Agreed?"

He looked round at each of his colleagues as he spoke. Slowly, they nodded.

"Agreed," said each of them in turn.

Harry slowly gathered his papers together and watched as his colleagues left the room. He hadn't been wrong. They had all known, right from the start, that it would have to end. The chances of getting another epsilon semi moron like Dick as Chief Executive was non-existent. The new Chairman of Trustees would presumably require more than one functioning brain cell for the top job. Even now, it still amazed him that Dick had managed to hold on to his position as long as he had. Mainly, he suspected, by agreeing with everything that the trustees said and never making any demands. And there was no denying that the Foundation was successful. Although not, he reflected, as successful as it might have been.

It still surprised him sometimes how it had all come about. It was as though the stars had collided. That Monday five years ago, after the usual tedious management meeting, they had all sat drinking coffee, reluctant to go back to their offices after Dick had bustled out in his usual little flurry of self-importance. They had sat and stared at each other, letting their drinks go cold. It was a cold grey day in March and ahead of them yawned the usual dreary routines. All of them were over-qualified for the jobs that they were doing. But just as they were all over-qualified, all of them were also considerably overpaid. None of the work was exactly challenging and the benefits were good. In addition to a considerable salary, a very decent company car and health insurance, all of them enjoyed considerable freedom; the latter on the basis that Dick never actively involved himself in anything if he could avoid it. Dick's abiding principle seemed to be that if he never did anything then he never got anything wrong, which meant that they pretty much had carte blanche to do as they liked. As long as the Foundation continued to turn a healthy profit while maintaining the aims of the deed of trust, there were no questions asked. The chances of any of them getting another job like the ones they had now were roughly nil and they all knew it.

He couldn't remember now who had first raised it. It had been said as a joke, a throwaway remark. Wasn't it strange how little scrutiny there was of the actual purchase of the properties? The trustees occasionally asked how the building or renovations were going or how many tenants they now had, sometimes they even enquired as to how the outreach work was going, but they never actually inquired into the purchasing process. And the remark had dropped into the silence that followed like a tiny raindrop into a small still pond.

8

———————

JEREMY DIPPED his head and sipped at his beer, looking around him over the top of the glass. The lounge bar of the hotel was filled with Christmas shoppers, their bulging bags bunched around their feet and their expressions tired but happy. From behind the bar the joyful shouts of Slade belted out. Here it is, Merry Christmas, everybody's having fun. Jeremy felt his spirits lift. He loved all these Christmas songs. When he had been teaching at Sir Frank's, Christmas had always been the best time of year. Lessons were more or less suspended and all the kids were allowed to bring in games, although he had been obliged to explain to his Year 10 tutor group that although poker was indeed a game it wasn't the kind of game that the staff had in mind. They had retaliated by deciding to play Pin The Tail On The Donkey at break time, having first unanimously elected William Stuart as the donkey. The poor kid hadn't been able to sit down for a week. He supposed that William ought to have been grateful that they hadn't decided to play Strip The Willow, an interesting variation of which Year 11 had devised.

He lifted his hand in recognition as from across the room a man stood up and waved at him.

"Jeremy, over here," he called, raising his voice above the hubbub around him.

Weaving his way through the packed tables he made for the table by the window at which Adam sat with the Chief Executive and the three managers. Moving around slightly and grabbing an empty chair from another table, he made way for Jeremy.

"Thought I'd invite these gentlemen for a pre-lunch drink," he said, smiling. "Try to get to know them a bit better. Glad that you could make it, too."

Dick smiled, a big genial smile that stretched across his florid face and made him look even more half-witted than usual. The managers, thought Jeremy, looked rather less pleased.

"So," said Adam. "They were just telling me about some of the things that they're working on at the moment. I'm keen to get involved. You were saying, Max?"

Max forced a smile.

"Well, there are several ongoing projects at present."

He fell silent.

"Such as?" Adam persisted.

Harry leaned forward, almost, but not quite, elbowing Max out of the way.

"There's a rather exciting new development that we're working on which may interest you. It's a new way of homing the homeless."

God, thought Jeremy. He makes them sound like rescue animals.

Adam beamed encouragement.

"Excellent. And what does that involve?"

Max cleared his throat and found his voice again.

"It involves building units from pre-fabricated materials.

They have little kitchens and bathrooms, a sitting area. And a bedroom of course. They're relatively cheap and can go up quickly."

"Like Lego?" queried Jeremy.

"Yes," said Max after a pause. "Just like Lego."

For several moments all six men sat silently. At the table next to them three women suddenly lowered their voices and threw furtive glances across the room. Jeremy strained to hear their voices and glanced with them. Perhaps there was a minor celebrity in town. He hoped so. It would be something to tell Molly and Carlos when he got home. He pulled himself back to attention as Adam spoke again.

"What about this other project?" said Adam. "Hightrees Place, is it?"

"Yes, that's right." Harry beamed at him as if he was the kid in class who had just put his hand up and unexpectedly and against all the odds given the correct answer. "It's a row of Victorian terraced houses. The plan is to renovate them and convert them into apartments." He turned to Max. "I think that the Foundation got it at a good price, didn't it?"

Max nodded, unable for the moment to speak again, his throat suddenly dry. He dipped his head and took a sip of his beer. Nigel remained silent.

"So how do you decide which properties to buy?" asked Adam. "I guess that they must meet certain criteria?"

Max nodded and dipped his head to his beer again, unable to look Adam in the eye. Yes, he thought. All the properties met certain criteria. The main one being that they were unsellable to anybody else, like being built on flood plains or having suffered subsidence. That was how their company got them so cheaply. And when it came to surveys, well, that wasn't a problem. There were bent surveyors, just like there were bent everybody else. And the trustees, keen to show what good business men they were in saving the Foundation money, chose to rely on those surveys.

"So, how do you find them?"

"In a number of ways," said Harry smoothly. "Our properties are spread all over the country. We have contacts among property developers that let us know if they've acquired a property that might be suitable and then one or more of us goes and inspects it. Of course, everything is put before the trustees."

Not quite everything, thought Max.

"Oh, I see." Adam paused for a moment. "I did notice when I was going through some of the documents from last year's meetings, that the Foundation seem to deal quite a lot with one particular company when purchasing properties."

Was it Jeremy's imagination or had the temperature dropped slightly?

———

JEREMY STIFLED A YAWN. He hadn't been wrong when he'd predicted that the annual lunch was going to be boring. He'd been at more interesting education conferences than this, and that was saying something. He looked at the flushed faces of his fellow trustees and the Foundation managers, arranged in a group at the top of the table. He hoped that none of them were thinking of driving. The wine had been flowing freely for the last two hours. Molly had dropped him off on her way to the supermarket but he'd already phoned her and told her that he'd walk home, the fresh air would clear his head and do him good. He gave a surreptitious glance at his watch. He was looking forward to this evening at home with Molly and Carlos. Molly had found the DVD of White Christmas at the bottom of the box of Christmas decorations and Carlos had promised to make some mulled wine and mince pies. If they were anything like the ones he'd made last year, they were in for a treat. There was no doubt about it, the boy was exceptionally talented in the kitchen.

He scraped his spoon around the last of his dessert and sat back. Had he imagined it or had he been correct in thinking that the managers had looked less than delighted when Adam had been asking them about the business of the Foundation? Not Dick though. Dick had maintained the same genial air of the intellectually challenged that he always wore. It was his defence against the world. No, it was the other men. There was a tenseness about them, a defensiveness that was hard to explain. The way they were sitting when Adam was talking to them looked awkward. Even Harry, the most relaxed and urbane of men looked sort of slightly hunched up. They reminded him in fact of a bunch of teenagers who were getting a bollocking which they considered undeserved. He was probably over-thinking it though. They just weren't used to the trustees taking such an interest. From what he had gathered, the previous Chair of Trustees, Charles, had breezed in and out like visiting royalty and taken about as much interest in the day to day management and workings of the Foundation as he would have in a dead fly on a windowsill.

He looked across the table as Adam stood up and pushed his chair back. The faces of the diners were raised expectantly towards him as he settled his glasses on his nose and cast a brief glance at his notes. Even if he hadn't known that Adam worked in a senior position at a bank, that's the job he would have guessed at. It was something to do with the charcoal grey suit, the elegant glasses and the beautifully clean hands. He just looked like the sort of man that you would trust with your money. He wondered suddenly if people could guess what he did for a living. It wouldn't have been difficult when he taught at Sir Frank's. Then, like many secondary school teachers, he wore clothes that were comfortable and easy to clean. Suits and ties were strictly for the ambitious. But now…

He jumped and sat up straighter and began to listen attentively as Adam spoke, his voice mellifluous and steady as he talked of new beginnings being built on a solid past. His tone grew warmer as he spoke of the work of the Family Fireside Foundation continuing long into the future. He reminded them that while they must always remain true to the aims of the founder, Sir George Renton, they should be prepared for the adaptations that they must all make in order to ensure that the Foundation was fit for the challenges of the twenty-first century. It was his intention, in the near future, to set up a working group to establish exactly what those challenges might be. He finished by thanking the staff for all their hard work in making the Family Fireside Foundation the success that it was and promised to support them in every way that he could. Finally, he removed his glasses and looked around him.

"I suggest that we have a short break and then, as we do every year, we will honour our founder by raising a toast to him."

9

MOLLY FLEW through to the hall as soon as she heard the key in the lock. Hard on her heels came Carlos. Grabbing Jeremy by the arm, she propelled him through to the sitting room. Shrugging off his heavy overcoat and pulling his woollen scarf from his neck and handing them to Molly, he sank slowly down on to the sofa. He looked at them for a moment without speaking. After taking one look at his ashen face, Aubrey and Vincent jumped up and sat either side of him, watching with their eyes half-closed as the flames from the fire flickered gently in the warm cosiness of the lamp light. From the kitchen the comforting aroma of cinnamon and nutmeg drifted through the open door.

Molly stood with Jeremy's coat folded over her arm.

"What happened? All you said was that there had been an incident." Molly tried to keep her voice calm. "Are you okay? I tried to call you back but when you didn't answer your phone I was imagining all sorts of things."

Jeremy nodded slowly, still not speaking, and loosened his tie. He scratched slightly at his right eyebrow and frowned.

"I'm okay. I'm fine," he said eventually, and then lapsed into silence again.

"Why didn't you let me come and collect you?" Molly demanded. "I could have been there in five minutes."

"I wanted to walk. I needed to clear my thoughts."

Molly studied him, her head on one side.

"Can we get you anything? Would you like a drink?"

Without waiting for an answer, Carlos sped over to the whisky decanter and glasses which stood on a small table next to the Christmas tree. A wedding present from Jeremy's great aunt and only used at Christmas, the cut glass twinkled under the fairy lights. Silently, Carlos poured a large measure and passed it to Jeremy.

"It was dreadful," said Jeremy, finally. He took a small sip of his whisky and sat back. "Utterly dreadful."

"What happened," asked Carlos. "Can you tell us?"

Jeremy took another, longer, draught of his whisky and nodded, his shoulders visibly relaxing as he felt the fierce heat of the whisky flood through him. He normally drank water with whisky but today neat was just what he needed.

"Well, as predicted, it was all pretty boring. All the trustees and managers sat at the top of the table, all the office staff at the bottom. So much for everyone being in it together." He frowned. "You would have thought that the trustees could have made the effort. And the meal, when it arrived, was totally underwhelming."

"What did they serve?" asked Carlos, his culinary interest, as ever, not far from the surface.

"The usual," said Jeremy. "Dried out turkey, undercooked roast potatoes, thin gravy. Christmas pudding sliced from a pack. God knows what the Foundation paid for it, whatever it was it was too much. I'm going to suggest to Adam that next year..." His voice tailed off.

Molly leaned over and gently nudged Vincent out of the way. She sat down next to him and took his hand.

"It's okay. You don't need to talk about it now if you don't want to."

Jeremy sat up straighter.

"No, I do want to." He took a deep breath. "Anyway, we got through the meal and then we had the chairman's speech. It was pretty much as expected. What brilliant work the Foundation does for those in need, how many fabulous success stories there have been, how hard all the staff work to make this happen, and so on. And then he finished by saying that we must ensure that the good work continues into the future." He paused, his expression bleak. "Then there was a short break, people started getting up to go to the toilet, going outside for a smoke, and so on, so everyone was moving around. Then everyone went back to their seats and we had the chairman's toast to the founder."

Jeremy fell silent again for a moment. Molly reached down and scooped Vincent up onto her lap. She sank her fingers into his rich dark fur and gently stroked his head. A small purr of appreciation rumbled up from his throat. Jeremy took a deep breath before continuing.

"A waitress brought in the claret jug and a glass. Adam filled the glass, raised a toast and took a big mouthful." He stared at Molly and Carlos for a moment before continuing. "Then everybody raised their glasses and we all drank to the founder."

"What happened after that?"

"People just started chatting and finishing their drinks. A couple of the office staff left because they had to pick up their kids from school. Everything seemed sort of relaxed. Anyway, after a bit most people started collecting their coats and so on. Adam was talking to one of the trustees and topped up his wine glass from the claret jug."

Jeremy fell silent and stared at the fire as if to ensure that he conjured up the right images.

"And then," he continued, "Adam got up to go too, he still had some wine in his glass but he reached down to put his glass on the table, and then he seemed to get very pale in the face."

"What, like he was ill?" asked Carlos.

Jeremy nodded.

"He collapsed. The glass fell out of his hand and he just sort of folded."

"What did the trustees do?" asked Molly.

"Nothing. Just sat there gawping like a load of stuffed trouts. One of the trustees had half-risen to go, and he just froze. I've never seen anyone actually do that before," he added. "Just freeze like that. It was almost comical. Except that it wasn't. Anyway, I tried to get up out of my chair to help Adam but I was caught between two of the trustees, neither of whom seemed able to move. Fortunately some of the office staff seemed to have a bit more about them. One of them is a qualified first-aider and she rushed over and started CPR and one of the other staff called an ambulance on her mobile. It seemed to take ages to arrive, although it probably didn't. It was just like time had sort of stood still. You know, like you read about."

"Will he be all right?" asked Carlos.

"I don't know," said Jeremy. "To be honest, he didn't look too great when they took him out."

"What was it?" asked Molly in a voice not much louder than a whisper. "Was it a heart attack or some sort of seizure or what?"

Jeremy shrugged, his face still pale.

"I don't know," he repeated.

———

Aubrey and Vincent turned left into Fireside House. Leaving Molly, Jeremy and Carlos to talk over the incident at the hotel, they had decided to get some fresh air before fresh snow fell. There was nothing that they could do for Jeremy at the moment but they'd go back later and sit on his lap. Make a bit of a fuss of him, as Vincent had said. They made their way towards the imposing front door and looked around them. Watching from an outside window ledge, Eric jumped down to greet them.

"This way," he said, leading them around the side of the house. Aubrey felt curious. Up until now, they'd only explored the front, they hadn't got round to the back yet. This place was much bigger than he'd thought. He glanced at Vincent who was looking about him with equal curiosity. Crossing the manicured lawns, picking their way through the snow and passing through the trees, they seemed to be heading towards a brick dome shaped building set among the shrubs and half-smothered with ivy. Small and squat, it would have been easily missed.

"In here," said Eric and disappeared.

Aubrey and Vincent looked at each other and then moved slowly towards a wrought iron rusted gate, tucked back and hanging drunkenly off its hinges. They liked Eric. They trusted Eric. But they didn't know him that well yet. Slipping round the gate, they stopped. Aubrey shivered.

"What is this place?" he asked.

"It's an ice house," said Eric, emerging from the gloom, and then fell silent.

Aubrey nodded, assuming what he hoped was an intelligent look. Thanks to the recent weather, he knew what ice was. But why would they keep it in a little house like this? Ah well, the ways of humans were a mystery. They were very good at opening packets of cat food and providing warm laps to sit on and that, really, was what mattered. You couldn't really ask much more of them.

"It's where they used to keep the ice in the old days," Eric continued. "I heard the gardener tell one of the trustees when they had the garden party last year." He fell silent again. Aubrey and Vincent waited expectantly. It didn't do to rush Eric.

For several moments they sat in perfect stillness and regarded each other, their eyes slowly adjusting to the light. Around them the dank brick work of the walls felt cold and forbidding. It wouldn't do to get trapped in a place like this thought Aubrey. Instinctively, he scanned the length and breadth of the chamber, searching for an exit. True, the gate was open but as every cat knew, two exits were better than one. And three were better still.

As if reading his thoughts, Eric finally spoke.

"It leads out into a tunnel." He nodded towards the far wall where a narrow opening was just visible. He paused again. "And the tunnel leads into the basement of the house."

10

AUBREY AND VINCENT scrambled up the last of the basement steps and edged their way round the fire extinguisher that propped the door open. Their paws sank into soft thick pile carpet, a stark contrast to the cold stone of the basement steps. The dim light, which was always left on in the reception area, lit the deep comfortable armchairs grouped around a low elegant table on which, fanned out in display, sat a number of glossy brochures. The air held a scent of lavender furniture polish that tickled across their nostrils. Eric looked around him with a faintly proprietary air.

"So, do you live here?" asked Vincent.

"Sometimes," said Eric.

"Right," said Aubrey, and nodded. "So where else do you live?"

"Here and there," said Eric. He turned suddenly and veered right, taking them into a large room dominated by a mahogany table grouped around by elegant chairs. "This is where they do their talking and stuff."

"Don't you ever worry about getting shut in?" asked Vincent.

Eric shook his head.

"No. Somebody always opens a door eventually. And there's the passageways."

"The what?" asked Aubrey.

"Passageways," said Eric. "I found them by accident one day. When I was exploring," he added.

He turned and padded across the room. He pressed against the panelled wall with his back and leaned his full weight into it. Stretching up he raised a barely noticeable wooden latch with his right paw. Aubrey and Vincent watched in astonishment as the panel slowly swung back and revealed a narrow dusty stair case.

HARRY FELT the sweat prickle under his arms and pulled the bottle of whisky from his desk, thankful as always that he had chosen to keep one of the old Victorian oak desks for his office, with all its little secret drawers and cupboards, rather than one of the big new designs that the general admin office was fitted out with. It was perfect for keeping items from prying eyes. Such as his whisky. He'd never asked but he suspected that drinking on the premises was something that Dick wouldn't approve of. He could be annoyingly puritanical at times.

In all his previous jobs, the drinking culture had been firmly embedded. It was when all the best deals were done, and the most productive alliances formed. Although those big boozy lunches were just a thing of memory now, he still kept a bottle of whisky to hand. Just in case of moments of crisis. Like now. He took a swig and then reluctantly pushed the bottle back. He'd already had plenty of wine at the lunch and whatever happened now, he had to keep his head. He chewed gently on the side of his thumb. Had he been a fool to come back here? Originally he had planned to sort it out next week but he had to do it at some point and it was better to act now while there was nobody around. With the offices closed up for the day when they all went off for the lunch, they would remain empty until the next morning. All things considered, there wouldn't be a better time.

He started suddenly at the sound of a small scuffling noise. It sounded like it was coming from behind the panelling. He swallowed hard. Mice probably. This old house was full of them, scuttling around behind the walls. Every two or three months Dick arranged to have them cleared out but they always came back. But nobody had returned to the building today, he was sure of it. He had left his office door wedged open and he would have heard a car pulling up or a door being unlocked. It couldn't be any of the office staff anyway. Only he and the other senior managers knew the security code and they took it in weekly turns to open up in the morning and to lock up and set the alarm when the building was emptied for the day. Setting the security rota, along with rodent control, was one of the few things that Dick managed efficiently.

H pulled the whisky bottle out again and took another swig. He had to give it to Dick, he was very good at the minutiae of office life. A stickler for time-keeping where the admin staff where concerned, he made it a point of honour to always be strictly on time in the morning. By the same token, he left every evening on the dot of five unless he was on the locking up rota, in which case he left at ten past five. Really, thought Harry, Dick had been born into the wrong era. He had as about as much idea of modern office life as he did about neurosurgery. Actually, probably rather less. He probably thought that the concept of flexitime or working from home was some kind of communist plot.

He sank down at his desk, the whisky bottle still in his hand, and stared ahead of him. The scene at the hotel had been like something out of a film, made even more surreal by the dropping of the glass that Adam had been holding. The claret left in it had arced upwards, seemingly in slow motion, and then spilled out in a great blood red splash across the white table cloth. For a moment they had all stared at it as though mesmerised. Then total chaos had broken out, with people barging about and shouting; the manager of the hotel, a small excitable man, had rushed in and began ordering people about, arms waving and voice raised. Luckily nobody had taken any notice of him. The arrival of the ambulance crew, one big burly man and one small capable looking woman, both with an air of calm authority, had restored order. Working quickly and efficiently they had tended to Adam and then taken him out to the waiting vehicle. The room had fallen silent as the wail of the siren punctured the air. With little left to do or say, most of the office staff had fizzled away and there had been just the managers and the trustees left. They had looked at each other and then one by one they had each left too. After Dick had volunteered to contact Adam's wife there had seemed little point in hanging around.

Putting the whisky bottle to one side, Harry unlocked the middle drawer of his desk. Pulling out a cardboard wallet, he flicked through the pile of PDFs. His heart sank. There were so many of them. Why had he printed them all? Even as he asked himself the question, he knew the answer. Because he didn't trust Nigel, that was why. It was all very well having an electronic system but that weaselly little bastard could turn black to white. He had wanted his own copies. Just in case. Well, that had come back to bite him because now he needed to get rid of it all, searches, land certificates, the company incorporation certificate, the lot. It would be fatal to have anything anywhere near him that connected to the setting up of the company or the purchase of the properties. The game was up. He'd pretended in front of Nigel and Max that there was nothing to get concerned about but, like almost everything else about him, that was just for show.

He stared down at the wads of paper in front of him. When they had been talking about naming the company, it had been one of the few occasions that there had been any real camaraderie between them. There had been an almost schoolboy hilarity in the room as they had each suggested more and more ludicrous names. In the end it had been Max who had come up with the name Henry Holdings Ltd. It seemed innocuous enough at first but, as Max had explained to them, Henry Every was a pirate who had made the most of his career within a very short space of time, amassed large amounts of money, and was most famously known for never having been caught alive. He had shown them an illustration of him on Google, a big ruddy man with a fierce beard and armed with the obligatory cutlass and pistols. How they had laughed. He felt suddenly sick. He wasn't laughing now.

He pushed the papers back into the wallet and stood up. What was done was done. The best thing now would be to shred the lot. He made for the door and then stopped suddenly. What if shredded paper could somehow be pieced together? Almost anything was possible these days. Also, the shredder was downstairs in the general admin office and it made a noise. Even though he was certain that there was nobody around to hear him, it was a risk not worth taking. It would be just his luck that Dick would walk in for something that he'd forgotten and ask him what he was doing. No, it would be far better to take everything away with him and burn it at home. He had trimmed some hedges recently so a bonfire wouldn't seem out of order. He half-smiled to himself. He was letting his paranoia get the better of him. Why on earth should anybody care or even notice whether he was having a bonfire?

11

Still holding the document wallet, Harry glanced ruefully down at his stomach. He was conscious that he'd let himself go a bit lately. His waistband was tighter and he was definitely more baggy around the eyes. Although he had pretended otherwise, he had been as anxious as Max and Nigel about the unwelcome digging around that Adam had been doing. As a result he had been drinking too much and eating crap food, often sitting up late watching old movies and drinking whisky while he thought about the best thing to do. It was starting to show. Well, now was the time to change all that. Once Christmas was over it would be the start of the new year. He'd go back to the gym, start eating properly, walk a bit more, use the car a bit less. He'd start some proper planning for the future, too. It had always been at the back of his mind to start his own agency. He had the experience. He had the contacts. And thanks to the Foundation and Henry Holdings, he also had the money.

He walked across to the window and stared out into the gathering gloom. Anxious as he was to destroy the papers, he was reluctant to go home to his empty house. It would be

Christmas in a couple of weeks' time and from where he was standing he could see the glimmering displays in the shops along the high street and the Christmas lights in the shape of stars and snowmen strung along the parade. The shoppers hurried along with their packages, coats buttoned up to the neck, each keen to get home before the snow started falling again. He stared down at them, feeling suddenly lost and forlorn. What would it feel like to be one of them? To be going home to a loving family and a hot meal?

Against his will, an image of his last childhood Christmas at home formed at the forefront of his mind, the jagged pieces slowly assembling into the dismal whole like a grim kaleidoscope. His father, a kindly man but with a habit of robbing banks at gun point, had left them some years previously and he and his brother and sister had known that for all intents and purposes Christmas for them that year would be much the same as any other year. A non-event. He had tried; he had bought his sister and brother little presents with the money that he earned from his paper rounds and which he kept hidden inside a small piggy bank that was actually shaped like a bank, given to him by his father, with no apparent sense of irony. He had even bought their mother something. A small blue vase from the market which she had stared at before placing it silently on the mantlepiece. And all of them had waited that Christmas morning, hearts in mouths, for the point at which their fat loud-mouthed violent mother had too much to drink.

When he had stared down at his mother's lifeless body lying on her stained mattress that Christmas night he had known that this ending was inevitable. Her flat dead eyes in her prematurely aged and broken-veined face gazed back up at him, the empty vodka bottle dangling from her cold hand. Even while he waited for the ambulance he had known that now they would have to leave the cold, meanly furnished and soon to be condemned tower block for good and he was glad.

It held nothing but bad memories. Tucked up on the sixth floor where the damp stretched its cold fingers out and touched almost every surface and the thin windows rattled in their cheap frames in response to the slightest wind, it had been all that the council were able to offer them when they had become homeless. To be fair, at the time he and his brother and sister had been grateful. That day they had returned home from school to find what few possessions they had out on the street and their mad chaotic mother reeling about in the road and shouting the odds with a landlord who was clearly at the end of his tether, had been the worst of his short life, and that included the time the police had dragged his father from the back of the wardrobe where he was hiding.

The first night they had spent in the local park, climbing over the gates after dark and hiding themselves in the bushes, surrounded by discarded syringes. They had gone into school in the morning, after washing in the public toilets, and they had all been glad of the warmth and familiarity of the classrooms and the opportunity to be children. Their mother, for once, had been sobered into silence by the consequences of her behaviour and had presented herself at the offices of the local authority housing department where she had been successful in gaining accommodation for them, first in a bed and breakfast and then the flat in the tower block. But the sobriety hadn't lasted. Within weeks they had arrived home from school to find her slumped on the sofa, mouth open and snoring, a faint tang of urine in the air. But that had been preferable to the times they had witnessed, shrivelling with shame, the sight of her staggering about and haranguing passers-by at the nearby parade of shops.

He had felt guilty about leaving his brother and sister in the care home where they had all been taken after their mother died, and if he could have taken them with him he would have done. But at least if they stayed where they were they would have a roof over their heads, which was more than he could guarantee if they had come with him. Being younger and cuter than he was, he knew that their stay in local authority care wouldn't be for long. They were nice children, in spite of everything that had happened. They were clean and polite and there would be no difficulty in placing them with foster carers or they might even be adopted. In any event, they would survive, as he would.

That night, he had watched the moonlight playing through the window in the room that the care home had allowed them to share. He had watched his little brother sigh gently and turn in his sleep and he had made up his mind. Swinging his legs out of bed and pulling on his jeans and T shirt, pausing to empty his piggy bank and stuff some clothes into his small school rucksack, he had crept down the narrow hallway. Silently taking the key from the cupboard in the hall he had unlocked the door and made his way down the stone steps and run out into the cold winter night. Without stopping to think, he had made his way to the place where he had been born and had spent the first ten years of his life. King's Cross.

12

———

He had been lucky, he knew. That had been in the days before the gentrification of the area, and many boys of his age hanging around a mainline station at night were quickly spotted. Friendly figures emerged smiling from the shadows, eyes narrowed, offering them hamburgers and chips and somewhere warm to sleep. It was only a matter of time before they were fed alcohol or drugs or both. And then pimped out to older men. Even at his age he had known that was a risk. While he didn't completely understand the ways of the world, he wasn't naïve. Being born into the family that he had been, any shreds of innocence that he had ever possessed had quickly fluttered away. But that night the Gods had been smiling on him and he had fallen on his feet.

On that cold winter night, wandering across the concourse and wondering what to do next, almost the first person that he had run into had been an old neighbour, Wanda. The things about her that had puzzled his younger brother and sister had not puzzled him. Her night work, the number of visitors to her door which seemed to be always men, the way the other women in the street avoided her, held no mystery for him. But he had always liked her. She was jolly and friendly, with a quick wide smile and always gave the neighbourhood children a few coins to buy sweets with when they ran into her. Once, she had taken him into her house and dressed a cut on his knee after he had fallen over. For which she had received a barrage of abuse from his mother and he had received a slap around the face so stinging that he had almost fallen over again.

Wanda had recognised him immediately and after buying him a hot drink and a sandwich, had taken him to the house where she said that she now lived. After a short consultation with the other women that lived there, he had been more or less adopted by them. Abandoning school altogether, he had run messages for them and brought them food, undertaken the cleaning and made them tea in the mornings. He had even taught himself the basics of a few dishes which he cooked in batches for the freezer. To this day, his shepherd's pie was second to none. Within a short time he had become invaluable to them. They had made him a little bedroom tucked up away in the attic which he had reached by a ladder and for the first time in his short life he had known what it was like to go to bed with a full stomach and without fear that he would be suddenly wakened by a foot kicking the door open and a screaming drunken banshee standing over him. His other main duty, selling to market traders the range of electrical goods which arrived at night and were stored in a small shed in the back yard, came easily to him.

He had stayed there until he was almost sixteen when, by another stroke of great good fortune, he was in the kitchen making pots of tea and putting together plates of custard creams and jammy dodgers for the punters, when the landlord strode in and started asking him questions about himself. Harry had seen him around before but he'd never actually spoken to him. At first he had been cautious, wary of giving away too much, afraid that somehow this man had the authority to have him taken away somewhere that he didn't want to go. In his experience, men in suits were generally in charge. He had given monosyllabic responses and kept his eyes firmly on what he was doing but the man had persisted until finally he had relaxed and had found himself sharing a pot of tea with him.

Tall and smart, always wearing beautiful clothes and smelling of expensive cologne, the man had fascinated him. After that first chat he had taken to dropping in to see him whenever he visited the women, and eventually he had offered him a job in one of his businesses. Just as junior office boy, nothing grand, but it would be a start. After consultation with Wanda and the other women, he had accepted the offer. Clubbing together, the women had bought him a suit and a tie and a selection of shirts to wear to work. Finding a small bed-sit which he could just afford out of his wages, and eating mostly sandwiches which the local supermarkets had reduced in price at the end of the day, he had begun his career in property management, moving several years later to an advertising agency and from there to public relations. It had all been remarkably easy.

Over time he had re-invented himself so completely that even the most curious would never find out where he really came from. Down to the smallest detail, nobody would ever catch him out. He had his back story ready but had discovered early on that he hardly ever needed it. People that he met assumed that he had born into a decent middle-class family, that he had received a good education and been to university. He never actually told them that he had but he had found that he didn't need to. It never failed to surprise him what people would assume given a few external factors, like a decent suit, a well-modulated voice and an air of complete self-assurance. That, and a good business track record, had given him everything that he needed to succeed.

He felt a sudden spurt of anger. He was in danger of losing

everything and it was all Adam's fault. Why did he have to start poking his nose in? Why couldn't he just mind his own business, like all the other trustees? He had disliked him from when he had first set eyes on him, and his instinct hadn't been wrong. All that public school confidence, that hail fellow well met stuff. He would bet that Adam had never had to strive for anything in his life. It would all have just been handed to him and he would have accepted it as his right. It would never have occurred to the likes of Adam that it was all a matter of luck, that even in modern Britain, life chances were still pretty much determined by the family that you were born into. And now there was that Jeremy, too. How much had Adam talked to him, he wondered. He gripped the document wallet that he was holding harder. Well, he had made his own chances. Why should he let posh twats like them take away everything that he had worked for? Worked damned hard.

He pressed his lips firmly together. What harm were the three of them doing anyway? The Foundation got the properties and the rents from them. The homeless got a home. To all intents and purposes these were victimless crimes. It's not like he was following the family tradition and going round holding people at gun point. He glanced at his watch. It was getting late. He needed to get a move on. The sooner these documents were destroyed, the better he would feel.

The three cats emerged silently on to the landing, cobwebs hanging from their fur. They watched as the man hurried down the staircase, a cardboard wallet folder under his arm.

13

JEREMY CAME DOWNSTAIRS from his study and strolled into the kitchen. Molly, sheet of paper in hand, was testing Carlos on the main vitamin groups in preparation for a college test in the morning. A text book on nutrition lay on the table before them. At least his upset about Teddy taking a gap year, as told to him by Molly, hadn't distracted him from his college work. He watched them both for a moment, her small blonde head and his dark one bent towards each other across the table. His mind slid back to the time when Carlos had been in his tutor group at Sir Frank Wainwright's. A shy easily influenced boy, nobody was quite sure where he had come from. He had arrived at the school one day with his Brazilian mother and been enrolled. His mother having been asked for details regarding his previous school, had simply ignored the question and left Carlos with the school secretary. When Jeremy had been summoned to collect him he had seen an underweight boy with badly cut hair, cheap trainers, and a uniform that was clearly second-hand and didn't quite fit him. Joining the school mid-year, he had been alone and friendless. Which was how he had come to fall in with that little shit Jed Caparo who had led him and another boy into trouble. Looking at him now, it was hard to believe. Tall and strong with a confidence in his future that a secure home can bring, Carlos was almost unrecognisable.

He felt in his pocket as his mobile began to vibrate. Sliding his thumb across the screen he walked through to the sitting room to answer it. Five minutes later he returned, his expression grim.

Molly and Carlos looked up.

"Who was it?" asked Molly.

Jeremy ran a tongue over his lips which were suddenly dry.

"It was Dick, the Chief Executive of the Foundation," he said slowly. He stared at them for a moment, his face blank. "Adam died an hour ago."

He sank down onto a chair and took a deep breath. From beneath the table where he had been contentedly listening to Carlos chanting food groups containing Vitamin E, Aubrey rolled onto his stomach and listened harder. Something was definitely up. That bloke that they had seen yesterday at Fireside House had looked distinctly furtive. It was the way he had slipped down the stairs, at one point looking back over his shoulder as though he was aware that they were watching him. The only time Aubrey and Vincent ever moved liked that was when they were up to no good. Like when they were slinking out of the airing cupboard after sleeping on the clean sheets and towels or nudging the tin of cat treats off the shelf so that it burst open.

Molly put down the sheet of paper that she was holding.

"How dreadful," she said. "Did he have a family?"

Jeremy nodded.

"A wife and two sons." He hesitated for a second and then continued. "According to Dick there's going to be an autopsy."

"What's an autopsy?" asked Carlos.

"Sometimes, if there's been a sudden death they try to find out the cause."

"What do they do?" Carlos pushed aside his notes on vitamins and gave Jeremy his full attention.

"They…" He faltered. Carlos's mother had died a sudden death. He hadn't really thought about it before but there must have been an autopsy. And there were some details that Carlos really didn't need to know. He had enough bad memories to last a lifetime, he shouldn't be burdened with any more. "It's like a sort of medical examination," he finished.

Carlos nodded. Jeremy, relieved that he seemed satisfied with the answer, continued.

"According to Dick, the hospital think that it looks like some sort of poisoning."

"Food poisoning?" asked Molly.

"Can't be," said Carlos, sitting back with an air of authority. "We did food poisoning last week. It wouldn't just affect one person." He thought for a moment. "Did you all eat the same things?"

"As far as I know," said Jeremy. "Apart from the vegetarians."

"And was anybody else ill?"

Jeremy shook his head.

"Not that I'm aware. But that's not all."

Standing up, he reached into a cupboard and pulled out a can of beer. Tearing back the ring pull he stood for a moment and contemplated it.

"Dick told me that the other trustees want me to take Adam's place. At least for the time being."

"What?" Molly looked confused. "Why? You haven't even officially joined them yet."

"I know. I said that to Dick. Apparently, they want somebody local, sort of on the spot, given what's happened, and I do have a lot of experience of meetings and committees and so on. They also want somebody younger. All right, Carlos," he added with a wry smile, "I mean younger than the current trustees. Their average age is over sixty at present."

Carlos smiled back and glanced at his mobile which lay on the work surface. He gathered up his notes and grabbed the phone.

"I'll finish this upstairs."

Molly and Jeremy watched him as he left the room.

"He's going to WhatsApp Teddy," said Molly.

———

AUBREY AND VINCENT nudged their way round the door and settled themselves on Carlos's bed. They watched as he sat at his desk and switched on his laptop. In seconds the image of a small girl with a heart-shaped face and blue and green strands in her dark hair appeared on the screen. They concentrated harder. They liked Teddy.

"Carlos. What's happening? Anything?"

Carlos shook his head.

"No, not really. I've got a test at college tomorrow. Oh, and some bloke that Jeremy knows died."

Teddy immediately looked sympathetic, her face crinkled in an expression of concern.

"Is he upset?"

Carlos thought for a moment.

"A bit. I mean like, he's a bit shocked and that, but he hadn't known him that long. He thinks that it might be poisoning."

Teddy drew in her breath.

"What, like arsenic and cyanide and things?"

Carlos shrugged.

"Nobody knows yet. They're waiting to find out. How's Casper?"

Aubrey nudged Vincent. Much as he liked Teddy, he liked

her brother Casper even more. He had been most disappointed when Casper had been banned from visiting them last time because he had been frightening kids at his school by getting drunk and pulling his blazer over his head and pretending to be the mad axe man. The impression had been considerably improved by the fact that he had got hold of a real axe and was waving it around.

Teddy sighed.

"Expelled again."

Carlos grinned, the lop-sided grin that lit his face and made Teddy feel slightly breathless.

"What for this time?"

"The education minister was visiting his school and Casper set off all the fire alarms. The fire brigade turned up at the same time as the minister. Mum said that she's at her wit's end."

For a moment silence fell between them and then, in spite of his determination not to mention it, Carlos said "You still going on that gap year thing?"

Teddy nodded, her pretty face lighting up in the way that always made Carlos's heart bump against his ribs.

"Dad's arranging it all. It's going to be great. Some of the others in my year are going too. We're all going to work in an orphanage and then we're going to travel around for a bit. And before that, we're going to do this mountain climbing thing, like camping out in tents. In Scotland or somewhere."

Carlos cleared his throat and pushed the word out.

"We?"

"Oh, Melinda. Jack, and Sebastian and a few others."

"Right."

He knew it. There were going to be boys there. And he knew what Sebastian looked like. Teddy had sent him a video of the school summer barbecue and she had been dancing with him. A sort of wild flinging about of limbs which Teddy had looked as though she was enjoying far more than Carlos would have liked. And that bastard Sebastian had at one point grasped her around the waist and spun her round, his stupid, thick, fair hair tossed from his face and then falling perfectly back into place, while his long legs clad in their exquisite designer jeans kept beat with the music. He swallowed hard and blinked.

"Teddy, I'd better go. I've still got to revise for the test tomorrow."

"Oh. All right." Teddy looked confused. "Speak tomorrow?"

Carlos nodded and quickly shut down the app. Moving across to the bed he lay down and gathered the cats to his chest. Burying his face in Aubrey's rich fur, his shoulders began to shake.

14

————

Nigel pushed his mobile back into his pocket and walked
through to the hall, deep in thought. So, according to Dick,
Adam was dead. He had survived the ambulance journey but
the hospital hadn't been able to save him. Climbing the stairs,
he ran the events of the Christmas meal over in his mind again.
When they had gathered for pre-lunch drinks at the hotel, he
had deliberately said very little. What his father used to call
keeping his powder dry. Let the others run off at the mouth if
they wanted to. Not a great chatterer at the best of times, he
had been determined to say as little as possible and he had
succeeded.

He walked into the tiny third bedroom which served as his
study and switched on his laptop. Downstairs he could hear his
wife Ava preparing dinner. He wondered what culinary delight
she would come up with tonight. He smiled ruefully. He was
very fond of her but a good cook she was not. Her last effort at a
Bolognese looked like something that the corporation would
scrape off the pavement after a bank holiday weekend. But he
wasn't complaining, he wasn't much of a cook either. Anyway,
he hadn't married her for her skills in the kitchen. She had other

qualities which had drawn him to her. The chief among them being a lovely face, a warm generous personality and a complete belief in him. Unlike other wives might have done, she never asked him awkward questions such as why he had to work so much in the evenings. She just accepted what he did without question. Amiable and loving, she was the most important person in the world to him and she would reap the rewards of his hours spent on the laptop, even though she didn't know it yet.

He ran his eye over the spreadsheet. The figures were stacking up very nicely. He'd invested the money well, the others had been right to trust him. Even when divided among all of them, it was still a considerable amount. Of course, he had hoped for one more year. One more year at the current rate of growth so that he could have his heart's desire and then some but even if they ceased all activity now, and it was looking increasingly like they would have to, he would still have enough to achieve his dream. Barring any disasters, such as a crash of the global economy, it was all now well within his grasp.

He sat back and folded his hands behind his head. Now that the kids were grown up and off living lives of their own, he and Ava could buy their narrow boat and start on their adventures. Goodbye office life. Hello waterways of Britain. He let his mind drift as he let the familiar scenario play out. Floating gently down the Grand Union, they would wave casually to the other boat people with whom they would be on first name terms. They would walk hand in hand along the tow paths and smell the wild flowers. They would enjoy drinks on board in the evening sun and meals at little country pubs. He had it all planned out. Winters would be spent in a pretty cottage that they would buy, or possibly a modern apartment with good access to bars and restaurants, he hadn't decided yet. And every summer on the boat. Life would be everything that he had always wanted. And he need never see Dick, Max or Harry again.

He considered his colleagues for a moment. He'd never really thought about them much before. They were incidental to his life. A means to an end, really. Dick was more or less irrelevant anyway, even the office staff pretty much ignored him except when he lost his temper over some petty incident and his face turned scarlet. Then, a cloud hung over Fireside House and they all kept their heads down. The last time had been when he had arrived late after a dentist's appointment to discover that a visitor had parked in his reserved parking space instead of using the spaces marked out for visitors. He had sulked for hours and nothing that anybody could do was right, from the senior managers down to Annie, the tea lady. Harry and Max were, however, another matter altogether.

For the first time he wondered what plans they had made, if any. He had never discussed it with them. Or anything else much, if it came to it. As far as he was concerned they were simply instrumental in his own plans. While he generally preferred to take the lone path, in this venture he had needed them. Dick might be seemingly oblivious to the day to day purchasing of properties, but he couldn't say the same of Max and Harry. Anyway, even though he was the manager with the overall responsibility for finance, they all needed to sign off on deals. He knew what they thought of him though. They thought he was a little grey man who wore little grey suits and who actually liked computers. If only they knew. He hated the bastard things. He'd only started working with them because that was where the opportunities were when he left school. But he'd kept his head down. He'd made his way. When the vacancy was advertised at the Family Fireside Foundation it had seemed like a good idea. Near where he lived, easy work and a good salary. He had also been given his own office and, as he quickly discovered, nobody interfered. At least until now.

On a positive note though, the immediate danger, Adam, was now removed. Utterly and irrevocably. But that still left the new trustee, Jeremy, with whom Adam had seemed worryingly friendly. Dick had told him that, by unanimous vote, Jeremy had been invited to take over the role of Chairman of Trustees. It didn't take long to work out why. It was because none of the other trustees wanted the job. They might have had to actually get off their arses and do something. But Jeremy had been there at that pre-Christmas lunch drink. He had heard what Adam had said. Had it meant anything to him? How much had Adam talked to him privately? There was no way of knowing. He gnawed for a moment on the side of his thumb as he mulled it over.

Closing down the spreadsheet tabs he switched to Google. Knowledge was power. Typing in 'Jeremy Goodman' he sat back and stared at the screen. Too many results. He thought for a moment. What else did he know about Jeremy Goodman? He was an Ofsted inspector, he was sure that Dick had said that when he'd told them about his appointment to the board. Quickly typing in Ofsted inspector profiles the screen jumped to the government website. Under the heading 'south east' sat what Ofsted termed pen portraits. And there he was. Jeremy Goodman. Qualified teacher. Considerable experience in secondary schools. Detailed knowledge and experience of curriculum development. He mulled it over. It didn't take him much further. He'd do some digging around. If there was anything to discover, he was the man to do it. And then he could put it in the locker, just in case he needed it.

He turned his thoughts back to Harry and Max. Could they keep their nerve under pressure? Not so much Harry. He had never seen Harry in a flap about anything. A big detached house, divorced twice and with a seemingly endless string of girlfriends, Harry appeared to sail through life with ease. Nothing seemed to bother him. Nigel didn't envy him though. He wouldn't want to swap places with him. He had pretty much everything that he wanted and he was more than happy. Ava and their little semi on the estate, which they had bought over twenty years ago and which they would sell for a lot more than they paid for it, was all that he required. No, it was Max that was the weak link. He had a tendency to overreact and the absolute worst thing that any of them could do right now was panic. They had to stick together, hold their nerve and beat a strategic retreat. He had wanted another year but if he couldn't have it then so be it. If necessary, he would simply cut his cloth according to his means. He always had done and this would be no different. But come hell or high water, he would have his dream. The smell of his wife's light floral perfume wafted through the door. Turning his head, he smiled at her.

"Dinner's ready."

15

———————

JEREMY CLIMBED the stone steps to the house and pushed the old-fashioned polished brass bell. He stepped back and looked up. The offices of the managers were, he knew, on the first floor. Had he imagined it or had someone been looking down at him and then quickly ducked back? He gave himself a little shake, he had to stop these thoughts. He was in danger of getting paranoid. But just lately, he'd had the distinct impression that he was being followed. A sense that he was being watched. He'd felt it again this morning as he walked to Fireside House. But when he turned around, there was nobody there.

He smiled at the receptionist as she opened the door to admit him. Whoever had appointed her had chosen exactly right. Of indefinable age, fresh and smart in her well-cut skirt and jacket, she looked like she had just stepped straight out of a nineteen fifties advert for the perfect personal assistant. She managed to be both competent and yet deferential at the same time. If this was really was the nineteen fifties then she would, he thought, have been named Valerie or Rosemary. Did people still name their children Valerie anymore? It was such a pretty name... he pulled his thoughts back to the present as Diana ushered him through to the main committee room. Seated at the big mahogany table were the Chief Executive and the three senior managers. He looked at their raised expectant faces. Dick rose to greet him, hand extended.

"Jeremy. Thank you for coming in this morning." He indicated a chair and waited for Jeremy to be seated. "And thank you for agreeing to take Adam's place at such short notice."

The three senior managers murmured agreement.

"I thought," said Dick, "that it was best for us to sit down together and discuss the situation in person rather than by phone or email. It is absolutely vital that we keep this amongst ourselves. We must not, under any circumstances, allow any unfounded rumours to sully the good name of the Fireside Foundation. It is, of course," he added as an afterthought, "a terrible tragedy and our heartfelt thoughts go out to Adam's wife and children." He turned suddenly to Harry.

"Did you send flowers?"

Harry nodded.

"But," he continued, "tragic though the situation is, the priority is, and must be at all times, to protect the Foundation."

Jeremy looked around the table at the sober expressions of the four men. "Has there been some kind of development?"

Dick drew in his breath and assumed a furtive expression, looking for all the world like a mourner at a funeral who has silently and lethally broken wind.

"Chief Superintendent Bickerstaffe is a fellow lodge member. I had a tip off from him last night. The police," he said, lowering his voice still further and drawing his eyebrows together, "have confirmed that it was foul play."

"When you say foul play..." said Max.

Nigel suppressed a twinge of irritation. There he goes, he thought, jumping straight in. Why couldn't he just shut up and listen? Everybody knew what foul play meant. He glanced across at Harry's smooth expressionless face. At least Harry had the sense to keep his mouth shut.

"They had the results of the autopsy last night," said Dick. "It appears that Adam had ingested a considerable amount of arsenic."

"But why?" asked Jeremy. "I mean, how?"

"That," said Dick sententiously, "is what the police intend to find out."

For a moment there was silence and then the door suddenly swung open and a small round woman, wrapped in a nylon pinafore, bustled in pushing a trolley before her. Wheeling it round she pushed it in a smart three-point turn manoeuvre, pulling up and parking next to the Chief Executive.

"I thought you'd be wanting coffee. Well, foul play you say?"

From behind the panelling where Aubrey and Eric had been listening, Eric nudged Aubrey.

"Annie. The tea lady. Dick hates her. And she hates him. He'd get rid of her if he could but he can't think of a good reason. She listens at doors," he added.

Aubrey looked at the rotund little figure with renewed interest, her face flushed with excitement. Listening at doors was behaviour in which they routinely indulged. How else would they find out what was going on? If they could read peoples' diaries, they'd do that too. Without waiting for a response, Annie lifted the big glass cafetière and began pouring coffee.

"I expect the police will be round asking us all questions. Bound to be. Surprised that they're not here already. Somebody must have seen something. I mean, we were all there. We all saw it happen."

She spoke with a kind of ghoulish relish, not quite

smacking her lips but almost. Dick looked at her with even more dislike.

"Collapsing like that. Right before our very eyes," she continued, rolling her eyes and laying a hand across her breast as though to calm her heart. "If you ask me, somebody knows more than they're letting on."

"Nobody is asking you," said Dick. "And I think that it would be better if none of us speculated at this stage. I would appreciate it, Annie, if you did not repeat what you have heard in this room."

"Good luck with that," said Eric. "It will be round the whole building before they've finished their coffee. She's all right, really," he added. "She takes in rescue cats and she always makes sure that there's some food out for me before she leaves."

Annie opened her mouth to speak and then closed it again as Dick cut across her.

"Thank you, Annie, that will do," said Dick firmly.

The two cats watched as Annie reluctantly left the room, casting a glance behind her as if to catch them out somehow. Aubrey yawned and stretched slightly. Neither of them were small cats and it was a bit cramped with the two of them behind the panelling. He was glad that he had come out this morning though. More or less confining himself to the house while the snow fell, it had finally stopped and settled, coating the garden with a thick white carpet and turning to slush on the pavements. For want of anything much else to do, he had headed towards Fireside House to see his mate Eric. He had no idea where Vincent was. He had disappeared around the time that Jeremy went out and hadn't been seen since. He pricked his ears as Nigel spoke for the first time, his voice measured.

"How do the police think that it happened?" he asked. "We all had the same meal and it was served at the table."

"Perhaps it was something he ate before the meal?" suggested Harry.

"I don't think it can have been," said Jeremy slowly. "Remember, we all had a drink together beforehand. He didn't collapse until at least two hours later Surely if somebody had deliberately done it, it would have taken effect before then. Particularly if it was a large amount."

"Perhaps it was an accident?" suggested Harry.

Dick shook his head in a decisive manner that made him look even more self-importantly imbecilic than usual.

"The Chief Super pretty much ruled that out when he spoke to me."

"Anyway," said Jeremy, "arsenic isn't the sort of thing you can casually pick up in the local supermarket. I mean, it's not like it would just be lying around in someone's house." He paused for a moment and searched his brain for any information that it might hold on poisons. The only things that he could think of came from his reading of Agatha Christie and right now that didn't really take him much further. "I mean," he continued, "don't you have to buy substances like that from a chemist and sign a poisons book or something?"

The four men stared at him blankly. They clearly didn't have any more of an idea than he did. Or, perhaps, one of them did? The thought flashed across his mind and he pushed it away. Annoying as she was, Annie had been right. There had been lots of people at the lunch, at least twenty five. Any one of them could have had something to do with this. But who? And how? And why Adam? The uncomfortable thought suddenly struck him that it could have been intended for somebody else, that Adam was the victim of what the law referred to as transferred malice. It was a concept with which he was actually familiar, it having been brought to his attention when Lennie Milroy, having been caught in the act of holding down Sebastian Thorn and punching him repeatedly in the head, had claimed that he had made a mistake and that he hadn't meant to punch Sebastian at all. It was Marcus Robinson who had incurred his ire by asking his girlfriend to sit next to him in English. Therefore, Lennie had claimed triumphantly, he wasn't guilty. It hadn't worked as a defence, with the result that Lennie had been suspended for two weeks. Which, to be honest, most of the teaching staff had regarded as a bit of a result given that on most days Lennie was not only determined to prevent his own learning but also that of everybody around him.

"I can't see," Jeremy said eventually. "Why it should have happened to Adam. He never did any harm to anybody. He was such a very ordinary man. In a good way, that is," he added hastily. "I mean, he was a member of my golf club."

He subsided into silence, aware of how ludicrous that sounded. Being a member of his golf club didn't make Adam a candidate for sainthood. Presumably even golf clubs attracted their fair share of bastards. But what he'd said in general terms was true, Adam was your all round general good bloke. Everything about him had shouted respectability, honesty and geniality. He was the sort of man who took his kids on exciting camping holidays when they were little and helped his neighbour to start his car on a cold winter morning.

"I should think that the police will want to look into his past and so on," said Dick. "There may be something there. We must bear in mind that none of this has anything to do with the Foundation. Obviously. We hardly knew him."

"But," said Jeremy. "It happened at the Foundation lunch. Clearly the police are going to be interested in all of us, if only for elimination purposes. And that includes the office staff," he added.

"I very much doubt it," said Dick, clearly annoyed that Jeremy had contradicted him. "Nobody else was ill. We all had the same meal. This is," he repeated, "nothing to do with the Foundation."

"There is one thing," said Jeremy slowly, "that Adam had that the rest of us didn't."

For a moment the silence hung between them as the five men looked at each other.

Jeremy cleared his throat before speaking.

"The claret for the Founder's toast."

From across the room, and heard only by the cats, came a faint creak from the door. Almost, thought Aubrey, as though somebody was leaning against it.

16

———————

DOWNSTAIRS in the little kitchen that had been fashioned from the old scullery, Annie busied herself washing the tea mugs. Scorning the dishwasher which stood in the corner, she carefully shook and then dried each mug before putting it away in the cupboard. She turned as the door opened behind her and Max came in. He strolled towards the First Aid box attached to the wall, hoping that it had been re-stocked properly. The last time anybody had recourse to use it, when one of the girls tripped over a trailing cable and sprained her ankle, it had been found to contain nothing but a card bearing the message 'Get Well Soon'. Dick had been apoplectic with rage. But at least he had appointed a proper First Aider.

"Got the most dreadful headache," he said, popping out two paracetamols from the pack and filling a glass of water from the tap. He tipped his head back and swallowed the tablets. He eyed her for a moment. He'd never really looked at her before. He wondered suddenly how old she was. Difficult to tell. She had one of those weathered faces that really gave little away. She was widowed so there was no husband to give an indication and he had never heard tell of any children so no grandchildren either. Some of the girls in the office had rather unkindly suggested that she was the housekeeper of Sir George Renton and had just mouldered on ever since. She had certainly been at Fireside House for as long as anybody could remember.

"They still at it down there?" she asked, her usual disrespectfully dismissive tone breaking into his train of thought.

Max nodded and handed her the glass to wash. In a corner of the kitchen Aubrey and Eric, who had now been joined by Vincent, hoovered their way around the food bowls that Annie had put down for them. He looked at them with an expression of pure dislike. One was bad enough. Now there seemed to be three of them. He gestured towards them.

"What are they doing in here? This is supposed to be a kitchen, not a rescue centre. There are hygiene rules to consider."

Annie turned to face him, crossed her arms and assumed her habitual expression of belligerence.

"They're not doing any harm."

Max considered her for a moment. This wasn't going how he had planned. Ignoring the cats who had now strolled over to Annie and parked themselves by her feet as if in a show of solidarity, he adjusted his tone and gave her what he considered to be one of his winning smiles. He leaned back against the wall, one hand in his pocket jingling the loose change.

"So what do you think, Annie?"

She looked at him suspiciously.

"About what?"

He tipped his head forward in a slight gesture of encouragement and raised one eyebrow.

"You know."

"No," she replied, determined to be unhelpful. "I don't."

The words rank and insubordination could have been invented for Annie. Singularly unimpressed by either status or seniority, she stared back at him. Aubrey shot her an admiring glance. He liked people like Annie. Jeremy could be like that, too, sometimes. Like the time he had faced down the irate neighbour at their last house who had blustered up to their front door and complained about Carlos kicking a football about in the garden which had accidentally banged against his fence, while at the same time letting drop that he was a local councillor. Jeremy had simply stared coolly back at him and then said finally, "how interesting" and closed the door in his face. He had warned Carlos to be a bit more careful in the future though.

Max smiled again.

"This business at the Christmas lunch."

"Oh, that."

Annie turned away and began unbuttoning her nylon overall.

Max felt his temper starting to rise and swallowed it back. Maybe this wasn't such a good idea after all. Much as he despised Nigel, he should have taken a leaf out of his book and left well alone. And he shouldn't have said anything about the cats. That was what had put her into un-cooperative mode. He toyed with the idea of stroking one of them and then changed his mind. The little bastards would probably bite him. The biggest one with the gold green eyes was giving him a particularly nasty look.

"Yes," he said. "That. What do you think about it."

Annie smiled. An annoying half-smile.

"Wouldn't you like to know."

Max resisted the urge to grip her warmly round the throat

and throttle the life out of her. That'd wipe the smirk off her face.

"Yes, Annie. I would like to know."

"Well, maybe I think something and maybe I don't." She hung her overall on the hook on the back of the door. "That's for me to know and for you to find out."

17

Jeremy finished his dinner, stretched his arms above his head, and sat back. He sighed with satisfaction and then drained his wine glass. Reaching out for a refill, he looked across at Carlos.

"Your cooking, Carlos, just gets better and better. I'm tempted to have a third helping. Except that I'd probably burst."

From across the room where Aubrey was finishing the scraps that Carlos had given him, Aubrey agreed. He couldn't work out what it was but it had a bit of cheese on top, and who didn't like a bit of cheese? He padded back towards the radiator and began washing his ears preparatory to a little refreshing nap. Where, he wondered, was Vincent? He seemed to have been gone for ages. Ah well, he'd turn up eventually. Never quite letting go of his need to be independent, Vincent still wandered off from time to time. Molly and Jeremy had learned to live with it now although the first time it had happened they had scoured the neighbourhood and put up posters on lampposts. When Vincent had returned two days later he had been astonished at all the fuss although Aubrey suspected that he had quite liked it, especially when he got double rations for dinner and a choice of laps to sit on afterwards.

Aubrey paused mid-wash and glanced up at Jeremy. He looked tired, his face pale and slightly drawn. The meeting this morning at Fireside House had upset him. He had returned lost in thought and looking troubled, and had spent the afternoon finishing a report that was due. Aubrey had kept him company by draping himself across the top of his desk but for once Jeremy hadn't taken him on his lap and had a little chat with him like he usually did. It was a pity, he thought, that Molly was on late shift at the Lodge. It was the sort of evening in which it looked like Jeremy could do with her calming presence. He turned his head as a light tap came on the front door.

"I'll get it."

Carlos loped through to the hall and pulled the door open. From the doorstep came the slightly tuneless strains of Good King Wenceslas. A small group of carol singers, faces pinched with cold and gloved hands pushed into pockets, stood in the porch. Smiling, Jeremy felt in his pockets for some change and handed it to Carlos as he put his head back round the door.

"Here."

Aubrey watched with interest. He didn't get this singing at doors business, and neither did Vincent. It always happened at this time of year and it seemed like anybody could just turn up, belt out a couple of numbers and then they got money. Weird. Or, he reflected, maybe they got the money to go away.

Returning seconds later, Carlos busied himself ladling a portion of the lasagne into a heat-proof bowl for Molly to have when she came home.

"Carlos," Jeremy spoke slowly and then hesitated.

Carlos stiffened and kept his back to him. Was he about to get a bollocking for something? Jeremy only used that tone when it was something serious. He thought quickly. He was sure he hadn't done anything. Well, unless you counted bunking off a couple of lectures the other day but surely it wasn't that? Everybody did it sometimes and he had needed to finish his assignment. Anyway, he had caught up on the notes from the college intranet. He turned and looked at Jeremy's strained face and his heart dropped. Was it something about Jeremy? Or Molly? Was Jeremy about to tell him something that he didn't want to know? Was one of them ill?

"You remember me telling you about Adam?" Jeremy continued.

Carlos felt his shoulders relax and sat down at the table opposite him. He nodded.

"What about him?"

"At the meeting this morning, Dick, the Chief Executive, said that the police think it was foul play."

Carlos crinkled his forehead, puzzled.

"Foul what?"

"Foul play," repeated Jeremy. "It usually means murder."

"What? You mean that somebody did it deliberately?"

"Yes," said Jeremy.

Carlos thought for a moment.

"What did he have at the lunch that nobody else had?"

Jeremy smiled suddenly and felt some of his tension disappear. With all the direct clarity of youth and dispensing of any need to express shock or horror, Carlos had gone straight to the point.

"The Founder's toast."

"Toast?"

Carlos looked confused. Who had toast at a formal lunch?

Jeremy's smile broadened.

"Toast as in drinking toast. You know, like cheers or bottoms up. Bottoms means the bottom of glasses, as in raising them. Not," he added hastily, noting the beginning of a smirk twitch around Carlos's mouth, "as in... anyway, do you remember me telling you about it before? Every year at the Christmas lunch, the Chairman of the trustees raises a toast to the Founder, Sir George Renton. The same jug is always used."

"Right." Carlos nodded thoughtfully. "Does anybody else drink from the jug?"

Jeremy shook his head.

"No. Because of its age, the jug is always handed very carefully and it's just the chairman that drinks from it. It's stored at the Foundation and only brought out once a year."

"So, where's it kept before the toast? I mean, is it on the table?"

"No, it's brought in by a waitress."

Carlos thought for a moment.

"What was the name of the hotel again?"

"The Mistletoe."

———

IN THE DEPTHS of Fireside House, not a breath of air stirred in the dank chilly depths of the basement. Watched over by the family of mice that had set up home down there, alone in the dark and without comfort, the body began to stiffen.

18

CARLOS PUSHED OPEN the swing door and looked around him at the bustling chefs and black uniformed waitresses. Blagging his way in by using the method that he had seen employed by his mother on different occasions, most notably when they had been out shopping and she had wanted to use the cloakroom in a hotel, he had simply strolled confidently through the restaurant and towards the kitchen as if he had every right to be there. Nobody had stopped him or even glanced in his direction. He turned towards one of the waitresses.

"Is Ella around?"

The waitress jerked her thumb towards a door in the corner.

"She's on a break."

One of the chefs turned to him as though to ask him what he was doing there, but spun quickly back around as the sauce on the hob bubbled up. Taking advantage of the distraction and moving quickly, Carlos made for the closed door and pushed it open. On an easy chair in the corner lounged a tall blonde girl reading a magazine, her long legs crossed casually at the ankle. At the sight of Carlos her face lit up and she sat up straighter.

"Carlos! What are you doing here?"

Surreptitiously she hitched her skirt up slightly to show more of her long legs and flicked her hair back behind one ear. Carlos settled himself on the chair next to her and leaned forward slightly, unconsciously sending a wave of Jeremy's cologne, to which he occasionally helped himself, wafting towards her. Ella dipped her eyelashes and thrust her chest out slightly. The subject of whether Carlos had a girlfriend or not had been the topic of much discussion among the girls in the student common room. Carlos gazed innocently back at her.

"Oh, I was just passing and I remembered that you were doing Christmas waitressing shifts here. I was wondering about applying for some part-time work myself." He bit his bottom lip. Did she know that he already had part-time chef work at the Lodge where Molly worked? There was no reason why she should but that didn't mean anything. Sometimes he thought that girls just knew everything. It was like some sort of magic power that they were born with. "So, what's it like here?"

Ella smiled.

"It's all right really. Pretty good, actually. The chefs are okay, at least they speak to you like you're a human being and they're not always throwing things."

Carlos nodded. A number of the students on his course had part-time jobs and some of the tales that they told of the chefs, even if half-true, meant that they should have had certificates, and not of the catering kind. It had made him determined that when he got his own restaurant he would never behave like that. Not even if the staff burnt all the sauces and dropped every dessert. Although, he reflected, he had to admit that some people were very annoying. Like that half-wit Barney whom the other students had nicknamed Rubble. He wasn't really stupid, he just didn't listen and as a consequence he managed to screw up almost everything that he touched. When he was in the training restaurant, he dreaded being on duty with Rubble. He had overheard one of the lecturers say the other day that he didn't know whether to talk to Rubble or water him, and Carlos thought that he had a point. But it probably didn't matter with Rubble. His old man owned a string of hotels. In fact now he thought about it, he might even own this one.

"And the money's not bad," continued Ella. "Even though we're only students, they still pay us a bit above the minimum wage. And there's lots of tips, because of all the Christmas lunches and dinners. I'll put in a word for you, if you like. I know that they could do with some extra hands, at least until the new year."

Carlos nodded.

"I heard that you had a bit of excitement here the other day? Some bloke collapsed or something?"

Ella suddenly sat up straighter, her air of studied maturity dropping from her like the façade that it was, and her young face suddenly showing the girl beneath who had only recently left school. She took a deep breath.

"God, it was awful. I couldn't believe it."

"What happened?"

"He just sort of wavered about and then he dropped. Like a stone. They took him away in an ambulance and somebody told me later that he died," she added.

"Were you on duty then?"

Ella nodded.

"It was one of the Christmas lunches. Foundation something."

"So what happened?" he repeated.

"Well," continued Ella, her eyes bright, "It was just after they had all finished eating and they were doing all those boring speeches and stuff. Then they had a break and they were all sort of wandering about, then they sat down again and I had to bring in this jug thing…"

"What?" Carlos interrupted. "You took the jug in?"

He bit his lip. Would she notice that he knew about the jug?

Ella looked at him, her eyes bright and her head slightly to one side.

"How did you know about the jug?"

"Oh, it was in the paper." He hoped that his tone sounded sufficiently casual and hoped even more that Ella didn't bother with the local papers. The only report that had appeared so far had simply stated briefly that a man had collapsed while attending a Christmas lunch.

Ella nodded.

"Well, anyway, I was standing near the door and I had to wait until the head waitress nodded at me and then I had to fetch the jug in from the kitchen."

"So it was all prepared beforehand?"

"That's right. It was on a silver tray on the side, with a little cloth over it."

Carlos thought for a moment.

"Who puts the wine in it?"

"The sommelier. None of us like him. He always stands too close. He really fancies himself," she added.

Carlos nodded in what he hoped was a knowing manner. He wasn't entirely sure what fancying yourself meant but it was a cardinal sin among Ella and her friends.

"When did he fill the jug?"

"He must have done it sometime in the morning because it was already full when the lunch started."

Carlos turned this thought over. If the jug had just been standing there, then anybody could have tampered with it. But commercial kitchens were busy places. People were in and out all the time, somebody surely would have noticed, although an idea suddenly struck him. The quiet time in a kitchen was when the last course had been served and cleared. There was a natural lull and people went off to have a break before cleaning down and preparing for the next service.

As it to confirm his thought, Ella said, "But there was nobody in the kitchen when I went to fetch it. The lunch had finished and everyone was taking a break until it was time to set up for the evening. Why? Why are you so interested?"

Carlos assumed what he hoped was a bored expression. Jeremy hadn't actually told him not to tell anyone but he had the distinct feeling that he wouldn't like it if he did.

"I'm not. Not really. I just heard about it, that's all."

"We've had the police round," continued Ella. "They talked to all of us."

"What did they ask?" said Carlos, trying to sound unconcerned.

"Just about what everybody ate and that. And they took some samples away from the bins."

"What about the jug?"

"We didn't have it anymore, it had gone back to the Foundation thing. Apparently it's quite valuable. You know, like hundreds of pounds or something," she added. "The police asked me about it, though."

Carlos felt his way cautiously. Ella was looking at him with some curiosity now. She was no fool. He didn't want her thinking that he was overly interested. Perhaps he had enough information for now.

"How did you do in the vitamins test?" he asked.

"All right. I passed, anyway. I prefer the online tests, do you?"

Carlos nodded.

"Yeah, somehow seeing the options sort of jogs the right answer."

Ella stood up and smoothed her skirt down.

"I'd better be getting back, they're busy in there." She hesitated for a moment. "Are you going to the college Christmas party?"

"Maybe," said Carlos, and smiled at her as he rose to his feet.

"I've just remembered something," said Ella, as she pulled a small mirror from her pocket and checked her reflection. "Something that the police asked me about."

Carlos felt his throat go dry.

"What was that?" he asked casually.

"It was a police woman. She asked me if there was anyone in the kitchen when I went to fetch the jug and I said no. Well, there wasn't. The manager was just going out of the fire door, I saw his back, but now I think about it, it can't have been him. I thought it was because he was wearing a suit, but he was too tall. The manager," she added with the classic teenage disdain for anybody that, in her opinion, fell short of perfection, "is a short-arse."

19

———

Harry fumbled in his coat pocket for the key. Only another eight days until Christmas and he would get a break from this place. And in the meantime he could get on with planning for the next stage of his life. It looked very much like it was coming sooner than he'd bargained for but that might be all to the good. After all, he wasn't getting any younger and there were bright young lads and lasses coming up all the time. They would be as hungry as he had been when he'd started out. That was the trouble with working at the Foundation, he reflected. While it was mostly tedious, there was no denying that it was comfortable. It had made him soft, complacent. There were no targets to strive for and no competition to beat off.

He realised with a sudden jolt of recognition that he'd missed that in his work. While in previous employments he had got heartily sick of hearing about performance indicators and key objectives, there was no doubt that they did concentrate the mind. Especially when there were others snapping at his heels and jockeying for position. The Foundation was the only place that he had been employed where there was no real impetus to succeed and no measure of failure. All he had to do was turn up and coast along. Well, he'd change that with the establishment of his own agency. See if he could find the old fire again.

He'd already started doing his homework. Spreading maps of England over the kitchen table, he'd searched for new towns. Or newish. Not too big, not too small. Like Goldilocks, he would know the right one when he found it. It would be somewhere where he could get premises reasonably cheaply and where there were lots of small to medium businesses that could use a good public relations and advertising campaign. And it would be so much the better if there happened to be one of the new universities nearby which might have students wanting to gain work experience. He couldn't compete with the big boys in the cities any more, he knew that, but he didn't really want to. These days he would be much happier being a big fish in a small pond.

He inserted the key in the lock and glanced at his watch. He was slightly late this morning. He had overslept, which was something that he rarely did. The receptionist looked up from her desk and smiled at him. Smiling back he began to slowly climb the stairs towards his office. Today he felt even less enthusiasm than he usually did. At least, he reflected, the police appeared to have finished with them. He half-smiled as he thought of Dick's outrage when they had turned up and insisted on questioning all the staff about the Christmas lunch. He had been even more outraged when they had refused to let him sit in on the interviews and had instructed Annie not to take them any tea or coffee. Typical Dick. Full of petty spitefulness, although what he had to be spiteful about God alone knew. As far as he could see, he had a pretty charmed life with a comfortable home, a nice wife and a job that required almost nothing of him. Which was just as well, as he had almost nothing to give. But Annie, being Annie, had not only taken trays of tea and coffee through to them but had put together a plate of the special foil-wrapped chocolate biscuits that were usually reserved for the trustees.

He reflected on his own interview. He had answered all their questions as best he could. Nothing, he had told them, had seemed amiss at the time. It had been a typical Foundation Christmas lunch, pretty much the same as any other year. Food, speeches, Founder's toast, then it was all over until it rolled round again. He hadn't noticed anything in particular, apart from the fact that one or two of the waitresses were very pretty. Afterwards he had just gone home. Which was true. He had gone home. After dropping in at Fireside House to collect the papers that he wanted to destroy. At the thought of the papers, he felt the familiar flutter in his stomach. He'd burned the papers, every last scrap of them, even raking through the ashes when he was finished to make sure that there were no legible words left. There was nothing on him now, either at home or in his office, to connect him with Henry Holdings. As long as the other two kept their nerve there was no reason why the police should go poking about in the affairs of the Foundation.

None of them had discussed their interviews with the police. They hadn't been told not to, but there was a sort of tight-lipped suspicious atmosphere that hung over the building and permeated every corner. The usual happy purposeful air in the general admin office seemed to have dissipated and Dick had been even more irritable than usual, keeping pretty much to his office and emerging only to bark some order at his poor long-suffering secretary. Why she stayed with him, he couldn't think. Probably the money, like the rest of them. Dick had even cancelled the weekly management meeting, claiming overwork, which would have been laughable if it hadn't been so pathetic. He climbed the stairs and glanced across to Nigel's office door. It would be good to know what the police had asked him. Perhaps he'd drop in for a chat.

Grasping the round brass handle, he put his head round the door. No Nigel. Glancing up at the old-fashioned coat rack, he could see that there was no coat hanging neatly on the hanger either. That was odd. He walked over to the window and looked out. Nigel's parking space was empty. He was never late and he couldn't be on leave, none of them took any holiday just before the Christmas break, it was one of Dick's rules. Everything had to be completely up to date before Fireside House closed for the holiday period and as the Foundation was very generous with the holiday allowance, allowing ten days for Christmas and the New Year plus a cash bonus, none of them complained. Perhaps Nigel was ill, although that would be very unlike him. Now he thought about it, he couldn't ever remember Nigel being off sick.

Two computers sat on a small desk to one side of the room, their screens dark. Harry would bet his bottom dollar that Nigel scrupulously logged out and turned them off every night before he went home. He sat down on Nigel's chair and glanced down at the surface of his desk. Everything tidy and in its place, just as it always was. Even his pens were lined up neatly on either side of the blotter on which Nigel had refrained from doodling. He picked up the small framed photograph which stood just off centre and studied the image of the smiling woman in the sun dress. Attractive, he thought. And somehow there was something sort of kind about that face. Something open and honest. Like newly baked bread. Lucky Nigel.

He put the photograph back down. Of the three of them, Nigel was the only one with a permanent partner, but if he had to put money on it, he'd swear that Nigel's wife was in complete ignorance of the activities of Henry Holdings. He glanced up at the clock on the wall. It was nearly nine thirty. Nigel was always at his desk by nine at the latest. Ah well, he was probably just held up somewhere. The snow had started falling again last night and although it hadn't fallen as heavily as before, it didn't need much to cause a bit of traffic chaos.

20

────────

Leaning back in his big comfortable office chair, Max chewed gently on his lower lip. Being on security duty he had come in early that morning and made himself a mug of coffee which now stood cooling on his desk. He looked around at his big airy office with its high ceilings and big windows. He had always liked working in the Fireside House building, it had been one of the things that had attracted him to the job. That and the large salary and company car. Having always worked in modern offices before, he liked the sense of history that the old building gave and he particularly liked his office. It appealed to the romantic in him. Given a choice and a better understanding of life's options, he would have stayed on at school and studied history at university. Or more probably art. But he hadn't had a choice. His father had made it clear that he expected him to be out earning his keep and so out earning his keep was what he had done. To be fair, it hadn't been too bad. Boring at times. Not exactly challenging. But all that had changed with the advent of Henry Holdings.

He closed his eyes. Henry Holdings. Not only had it provided him with that element of excitement that he'd never had before, it had been his passport to freedom. If it all folded now, which presumably it must, would he still have enough to fulfil his dream? Surely he would, particularly if he managed to get the old bag out of the house and sell it. A wave of something very like panic rippled across his chest. He had to make this work. One way or another. Come hell or high water, he wasn't going to let go of it now. It was the only thing that he had to look forward to. The alternative was a slow coast down to retirement and a diet of ready meals, day-time telly and elasticated waist trousers. No, he would stick to his plan. A one-way ticket to an island somewhere, he hadn't determined which yet because thinking about it was half the pleasure, and then spending the rest of his life painting, drawing and drinking wine. No more sitting hunched up in the little garden shed that he had converted into a studio, no more being interrupted by the old bag banging on the door wanting to know what he was doing in there, like he was watching a live sex show or something. He was planning for a completely new life. One that he had always dreamed of.

Pushing aside the unwelcome thoughts of Stella, he looked around him. Given where it was situated, he thought that his office had probably been a bedroom once. It wasn't as big as Dick's office which overlooked the grounds at the back and had presumably been the bedroom of Sir George Renton and his wife, but it was big enough. Certainly bigger than any other office he had ever occupied. Above him were the attic rooms, now largely empty except for old rolls of wallpaper, broken office furniture and defunct computer equipment. He guessed that they had originally been the bedrooms of the servants, giving access as they did to the back staircases behind the panelling so that the master and the mistress wouldn't have the inconvenience of running into them while they went about their work. So perhaps his office had been the bedroom of one of the children, or maybe a nursery, like one of those Victorian ones, with a rocking horse and a doll's house in the corner, the sort that loomed large in ghost films.

He closed his eyes and let the random thoughts soothe him. He had barely slept recently and his eyes were sore and itchy with tiredness. His insomnia hadn't been helped by his stepmother's night time activities. He would swear that every time he managed to drop off to sleep, she got up to use the bathroom. For a relatively small woman, she had a tread like an elephant and a bladder the size of Wales. It wouldn't surprise him if she was doing it deliberately. Relations between them had been even more strained than usual recently and he had started to dread going home. The nightmares had been awful too, the last one involving him being marched from Fireside House by Dick, prodded up the arse with one of those devil trident things and then pushed on to a bonfire with those bastard cats watching him, their eyes gleaming in the light from the flames.

He stood up and walked towards the big sash window, leaning his tired head against the cool glass. Normally when he felt like this he would make himself a strong coffee to get himself going but he hadn't yet drunk the one he'd made earlier. Perhaps he would go outside for a little walk, get some fresh air. Much as he liked Fireside House, lately it had started to feel claustrophobic, as if the walls were closing in on him. Grabbing his coat and scarf from the hook he walked down the stairs and out of the back door to avoid seeing the receptionist. Usually he stopped for a little chat with her, given that in her position as receptionist she had her finger pretty much on the pulse of everything that went on, but he wasn't in the mood for making small talk today.

Once outside he stood on the step and raised his head. The cold brilliance of the blue-grey sky was breath-taking after the artificial light in his office. He closed his eyes and took a great lungful of air, inhaling as deeply as he could, savouring the cold freshness of the light snow flakes brushing gently against his upturned face. He opened his eyes again and looked about him. The snow had placed a lacy white blanket across the plants and trees and he felt his spirits lift. Everything would be all right. It was always all right in the end. He just had to be patient and keep his nerve. He shoved his hands in his pockets and turned down the gravel path towards the shrubbery, enjoying the feeling of the snow crunching under his feet. Halfway along he stopped. Lying on the path in front of him was Eric, his thick fur matted with blood that had seeped from the wound in his side. The snow around him was stained a deep red.

Eric raised mournful eyes towards him. Even from where he was standing Max could hear the stertorous breathing, thick heavy rasps that forced their way out of the injured body. Max moved closer and leaned over. It looked like the cat had been attacked by something, perhaps a fox or a badger. He wasn't great on this nature stuff but it had definitely been something bigger than Eric. He hesitated for a moment, almost tempted to just carry on walking but it was no good. He couldn't just leave the creature lying here. He had the uncomfortable feeling that when the time came, he would have enough explaining to do at the pearly gates, without the added crime of leaving an injured animal to die. He'd take it in to the house and ask the receptionist to call a vet.

Slipping his scarf from his neck, he bent down and carefully folded Eric into it. It would stain his scarf but he'd never much liked it anyway. It had been a Christmas gift from his stepmother, the kind of gift that you give a man when you can't be bothered to think of anything else. Like socks and pyjamas. Anyway, given everything else that had happened, what did a ruined scarf matter? Lifting the injured cat, he cradled him against his chest for a moment and stared into the tragic little face, instinctively running a finger along his soft back. To his complete amazement, Eric gave his hand a tiny lick and settled against him, the small warm head nestled trustingly against his chest. A tiny but distinct purr rattled upwards. Max felt a sudden wave of happiness flood through him and his throat thickened. He hadn't had a girlfriend for ages and he couldn't remember the last time a living thing had voluntarily made physical contact with him, other than the obligatory hand shaking at meetings, and that didn't count. He swallowed hard and rested his hand beneath Eric's head.

"Come on, you little sod. Let's get you inside and fixed up."

21

———————

STILL HOLDING Eric to his chest, one hand rhythmically stroking his head, he strode through to reception. The receptionist looked up at him, her professional smile ready in an instant. Max leaned towards her.

"The cat's been injured."

Even as he spoke he felt foolish. It was bloody obvious that the cat was injured. He wouldn't have been wrapped up in his scarf dripping blood otherwise. The receptionist leaned forward and peered at Eric.

"Poor little thing. I'll ring the vet."

Even as she spoke, Max knew that he would be the one that would have to drive him there. The receptionist couldn't leave her station and he couldn't very well barge into the main office and demand that one of the staff take him. He wasn't even sure how many of them had cars. He thought for a moment. It would be better, and easier for Eric, to bring the vet out here. The Foundation would pay.

"Ask the vet to come here. Tell him it's an emergency."

The receptionist nodded and picked up the telephone. Max looked at her with admiration. Of course she had a vet's number in the phone memory. Of course she did. He bet that if he'd asked her to get the Pentagon on the line she would have simply scrolled up the number. She covered the mouth piece with her beautifully manicured hand.

"By the way, have you heard from Annie this morning?"

Max shook his head.

"No. Why?"

"She doesn't seem to have turned up yet and it's not like her to be late without telephoning to let us know."

He opened his mouth to speak and then turned as Harry descended the stairs.

"Morning Max. Seen Nigel around?"

"Not in his office?"

"No. His coat isn't there either."

"Probably held up by the weather."

Harry leaned over the bundle that Max was holding.

"What have you got there? Not old Eric is it?"

Max smiled ruefully.

"He's come a cropper somehow. I think that something might have attacked him."

"Looks like he's still breathing," said Harry, reaching across to stroke him. "I thought that you didn't like him?"

"I don't like Dick either," said Max grimly, "but I wouldn't leave him to die. Probably."

Harry grinned.

———

DOWN IN THE basement Lettie stared hopelessly at the dusty racks of files and deed boxes. Sent down by her supervisor Yvette to locate and fetch something called the Harrison files, she really had no idea what she was looking for. She ran a finger along the nearest shelf while she thought about it. It would help if the files were labelled properly and stored alphabetically but they all seemed to be stacked randomly, like they'd just been shoved back anywhere as soon as somebody had finished with them. Some of them had been computerised but not all of them. It was one of those jobs that always went on the back burner and was only addressed, and even then reluctantly, when there really was nothing else to do, which wasn't often. She gave a sigh, pulled down the first deed box and peered inside. It was too gloomy down here, she couldn't see what she was looking at. The only light was coming from the open door at the top of the stairs. She looked around. There must be a light switch somewhere. Common sense told her that it would probably be located by the doorway. Feeling her way towards it, she pushed down the switch.

Flickering uncertainly at first, the long strip light on the ceiling suddenly burst into life bringing with it a smell of burning dust. Lettie blinked against the strong white light and looked around her. A large lump seemed to have been pushed into the far corner. She moved towards it and stared down at the throttled mottled face. The screams, little more than breathless gasps to begin with, slowly built up into a crescendo that reverberated up the basement steps and out through the whole of Fireside House.

22

———————

Yvette leaned over the girl and held one of her hands while she smoothed the hair back from her face. Grouped around her stood several of the office staff who had come running at the sound of the screams. Lettie sat back in the chair and stared ahead, the pretty comb that she had put in her hair that morning had slipped and her eyes were wide. Her face pale, her free hand clutching at the glass of water that Yvette had given her, she took a slow steady sip. Gradually the colour returned to her face and she sat up straighter. Outside the sound of a car engine broke through the silence. The receptionist opened the heavy oak door to admit the vet, black bag in hand and a harried expression stamped across his face.

"Where's the patient?"

Before anybody could answer, Dick marched down the stairs and strode forward. He grasped the vet by the arm.

"I expect that you want to see the body. It's down in the basement."

Looking surprised, the vet followed Dick down to the basement only to remerge seconds later, his confusion evident. Trying to hide an inappropriate grin, Harry moved forward.

"Eric, the cat, is in the kitchen."

Gesturing towards the kitchen door, Harry turned as the receptionist pulled open the door again to admit a group of people who were definitely not vets and some of whom seemed to be wearing protective clothing. Suddenly the hall, which he had always thought quite large, seemed rather small. The tallest of the group looked around him, a lean spare man with keen blue eyes and an unmistakeable air of authority.

"Who's in charge here?"

Dick pushed his way forward, chest first and head held high, pointedly refusing to meet the eye of any of the staff gathered in the hall. He had just made a fool of himself with the vet and he knew it.

"I am the Chief Executive."

The police officer nodded.

"And where is the body?"

Dick gestured towards the basement door which, as always, was propped open. The officer nodded towards the men and women who had arrived with him and watched as they slipped down the steps.

"Is all this really necessary?"

The note of petulance in Dick's voice was unmistakeable. The policeman regarded him thoughtfully.

"That, Sir, is what we're here to find out."

"As I'm sure you're aware, I am a close personal friend of Chief Superintendent Bickerstaffe" Dick puffed his chest slightly and made a pathetic attempt to regain some authority. "Perhaps you would like to come up to my office. I will ask one of the girls to bring us up some coffee."

"No thank you, Sir. Not just at the moment. We need to get the scene secured first. And," he continued, "I would like to speak to the person who found the body."

The small group of people standing around Lettie parted.

She stared glumly up at the police officer who leaned down towards her, a kindly expression on his face.

"Was it you?" he asked.

Lettie nodded, her bottom lip starting to tremble again. The police officer turned towards Dick.

"Is there somewhere private that we can talk? And perhaps this lady," he gestured towards Yvette, "would like to come with us."

Still smarting from the earlier rebuff, Dick stared sullenly back at him and remained silent. Max moved forward.

"You can have my office, it's quiet up there."

"What's going on?"

Stamping the snow from his shoes, Nigel strode into the hallway.

23

THE THREE MEN faced each other across the table. From upstairs the sense of Dick sulking was almost palpable. Max raised his eyebrows and nodded towards the ceiling.

"Let's hope he stays up there. I could do without him huffing and puffing all over the place today."

From his lap, Eric gave a small purr in agreement. His injury had looked far worse than it was and once the blood had been washed away it had been easy to treat. Now, stitched and fed, he had started to follow Max about, limping along behind him like a small silent ghost. From beneath one of the winged back chairs, Aubrey and Vincent settled down to watch. Having made their way through to the basement from the ice house, only to discover it full of people, they had quickly slipped up the stairs to the main house. From behind the door they had watched, along with everybody else, as the black plastic body bag was carried to the waiting private ambulance. The hall had fallen silent in an instinctive and collective mark of respect as the sad little procession made its way out. When the phone had suddenly rung they had all jumped.

"Answer that bloody thing," Dick barked at the receptionist

although, like everybody else in the hall, she had barely had time to register that it was ringing. "And the rest of you," he gestured around the hall, "get back to work. There's no point in standing around being idle when there's work to do."

Dick had turned and stamped back up the stairs towards his office, slamming his door behind him. They had all stared at his departing back. Dick in a mood was nothing unusual but none of them had ever heard him swear before.

Shuffling the papers that they had brought down as a cover in case any of the police officers came in to the meeting room and asked them what they were doing, Harry looked at his colleagues. Although they had agreed to meet in a neutral space rather than in one of their offices, each of them seemed suddenly reluctant to speak. They eyed each other cautiously.

"Dick never liked her anyway," said Nigel, finally breaking the silence. "So he needn't bother shedding any crocodile tears."

"Well, one thing's for sure," said Harry. "He can't stop the police poking around Fireside House now," he paused. "But, you know, if that girl hadn't been sent down to fetch the files, the body could have lain down there for months. It's very cold down there."

Nigel opened his mouth to speak again and then closed it as the door opened and the senior police officer and one of his female colleagues put their heads into the room.

"Ah, there you are gentlemen. As you're all together, would you mind if I asked you a few general questions? Just about how the Foundation operates and so on." The officer's tone was even. Neither friendly or unfriendly. "So we can get a better picture of how things work. We shall want to talk to you all separately as well, of course."

The men nodded and watched as the officers sat down. The female officer took out a notebook.

"Could we start with the deceased? Can you tell us anything about her? Who she lived with and so on?"

"That's me," said Max. "I don't mean I live with her," he added hurriedly. "I mean I am, was, her manager."

The officer nodded and waited.

"There's not a lot to tell," said Max. "As far as I'm aware, she was a widow and lived on her own. She's worked at the Foundation for as long as anybody can remember. That's about it."

"And what exactly was her job, sir?"

Max shrugged.

"Making the tea. Sometimes she baked cakes for the trustees meetings. If she was in a good mood," he added.

"Right." The officer looked thoughtful. "Anything else?"

"She sometimes did some cleaning when one of the regulars didn't show up."

"And what is the basement used for?"

"Old files, mostly," said Nigel.

And the storage of bodies, thought Aubrey.

"Would Annie have had any reason to be down in the basement?"

"No," said Nigel. "Hardly anybody ever goes down there. The only reason that somebody might be there is to find one of the old case records. None of that was anything to do with Annie."

"What are the security arrangements here?" asked the officer, suddenly swerving direction. "Can anyone just come and go?"

"No," said Nigel again. "During office hours, anybody entering the building would have to go through reception and would also have to sign the visitors book. The back doors and French doors and so on are kept locked and can only be opened from the inside."

"I see." The police officer looked thoughtful. "Who has keys?"

"All of us," said Harry. "I mean, all of us senior managers."

"Anybody else? Any of the office staff?"

Harry shook his head.

"No."

"So no chance of anybody just slipping in?"

Harry shook his head.

"And after office hours?"

"That's on an alarm system," said Harry. "It goes straight through to the police station. Anybody coming in when the offices are closed would set the alarm off."

"But it has a code," persisted the officer. "Who has the code?"

For a moment there was silence. Aubrey watched with solemn eyes. When he and Vincent had emerged from the tunnel into the basement he had spotted the body straight away. Even through the legs of the people standing around, he had seen that it was Annie. On her back, her arms flung wide, her usually bright eyes were dimmed and her mouth hung slightly open. The absence of life was unmistakeable, it was as though the inner spirit had surged up and flown away, leaving only the deathly stillness of the husk of the body behind.

Annie's flowered nylon overall had been ripped away from her body, the buttons burst open. It was, he thought, as though she had been grabbed from the back as she tried to escape and had been overpowered. But why Annie? What had she ever done to anybody? He thought for a moment about the little woman whom both he and Vincent had become fond of. Weather-beaten face, with a faint smear of pink lipstick on the mouth and a brush of pencil on her brows after the fashion of her youth, she had always looked neat and tidy. Bustling about in the kitchen she had often sung along to the tunes on the radio which she kept on low, because Dick had decreed that radios had no place in Fireside House although listening to the cricket in his own office had obviously been another matter. And there had always been a little something for them when they had dropped by. Aubrey half-smiled to himself. If Dick had known that Annie frequently purchased cat food from the money allocated to buy provisions for the kitchen, he would have had a blue fit. But, as Annie had observed to them the last time that they had seen her, it's not like the Foundation couldn't afford it. And, as she had also rather astutely observed, Sir George Renton hadn't specified that charitable funds were reserved only for humans.

"All of us have the code," said Harry at last. "And Dick. But," he added, "Annie wouldn't be here after office hours."

"Are you sure?" asked the officer.

24

———————

A UBREY WATCHED from the bedroom window sill as Jeremy strode off along the road, one hand clutching Christmas cards for the post box which stood on the corner. Looking across the garden he could see Vincent picking his way across the snow-covered lawn, his large glossy black shape in dark contrast to the whiteness surrounding him. He had been a bit concerned about Vincent lately. He seemed to have been rather unsettled but not for any good reason that Aubrey could see. However, it was true that Vincent, for all his appearance of outward coolness and control, tended to worry about things. Ever since his previous owners had disappeared in what they had overheard called tragic circumstances, he had somehow never quite managed to take anything for granted. He was eating all right though, and that was the main thing. In Aubrey's experience, as long as a cat had the strength to turbo around his food bowl there wasn't too much wrong. He wondered where Vincent was going now. He had a very purposeful air about him but he hadn't said and Aubrey hadn't liked to ask. Wherever it was, he clearly hadn't wanted any company.

He turned his head as Carlos came in and switched on his

computer. Within seconds Teddy's pretty face appeared on the screen. Carlos smiled, the lop-sided smile that had, unbeknown to him, caused several hearts, both male and female, to flutter in the student common room.

"Carlos." Teddy eyes lit up and unconsciously she leaned in towards the screen. "What's new?"

"Nothing much," admitted Carlos. "I passed my vitamins test."

"Brilliant!"

Teddy's enthusiasm was obvious, her cheeks slightly flushed.

"It wasn't that difficult," he admitted. "It was one of those multi-guess things."

"Yes, but you passed," persisted Teddy. "I bet not everybody did."

Carlos smiled the lop-sided grin again. Teddy always had the knack of making him feel good about himself. And it was true, not everybody had passed. Rubble, for instance, had failed. And failed rather admirably, given the outstandingly low score that he had managed to achieve. As one of his lecturers had said, it took real talent to not only guess the answers but to guess eighty-five percent of them wrongly. Rubble hadn't looked as though he was bothered though. And, to be fair, probably nor would Carlos be if had a father who was loaded like Rubble's was.

"How's Casper?" he asked.

Teddy made a mock groaning noise.

"He's on his second home tutor."

"What happened to the first one?"

"Casper told him that he was studying the effect caf poisons on humans and showed him a little bag of powder." She paused. "And then he asked him if he would like a cup of tea."

Carlos laughed.

"What was really in the bag?"

"Some dishwasher tablets that he opened."

"Talking of poisons," continued Teddy. "What happened about that friend of Jeremy's?"

"Jeremy told me that the police think it's foul play." He said the words with a slight air of self-consciousness, proud to have extended his vocabulary in such an interesting way. He felt a twinge of disappointment when instead of Teddy asking him what he meant, she simply nodded.

"Right. Do they know what it was?"

"Jeremy thinks that maybe it was arsenic, he looked up the symptoms, but he doesn't know how somebody would get hold of it. I mean, like, I don't think that you can just go and buy it or anything."

"The internet probably, you can get anything on there," said Teddy. "But I'll ask Casper. I bet he knows. Does anybody know how it was done?"

Carlos nodded, his face serious.

"Probably at the Christmas lunch. They always have a special toast to the founder. And they use this special antique jug thing. The only person that drinks from it is the chairman of trustees so Jeremy thinks that must have been how it happened."

"Right." Teddy nodded. "So who had access to the jug?"

"That's what I asked Ella," began Carlos eagerly. "And she said..."

"Who?"

Teddy's voice was suddenly cold. Her small face stony.

"Ella," said Carlos uncertainly.

"Who's Ella?"

"She's a catering student at college. She's on my course and she works in the hotel where it happened so I went to see her and..."

"What's she like?" Teddy interrupted.

"She's nice," Carlos replied. "Friendly."

Teddy's small mouth twisted in an unmistakeable expression of contempt.

"I mean, what does she look like?"

"Sort of tall with long hair. Blonde," he added.

"I see. I have to go now, Carlos."

And with that she disappeared from the screen. From the window sill Aubrey watched as Carlos turned a forlorn face towards him.

"What did I say?" he asked miserably.

Have a little think about it, thought Aubrey. Teddy was small, dark-haired with green and blue highlights and very pretty indeed. But tall and blonde she was not.

"Do you think that Teddy's upset?"

That, considered Aubrey, was an understatement. Teddy had looked like a thunder cloud that was about to erupt. Lovely though Teddy was, he had the feeling that he wouldn't like to be on the rough side of her tongue. She might be small but she was a force to be reckoned with. On one or two occasions even Casper had been known to behave himself when Teddy told him off.

Carlos scooped him off the window sill and sat down on the bed, clutching him to his chest.

"Do you think it was because of what I said about Ella?"

Only totally, thought Aubrey, trying to wriggle free so that he could breathe.

"But Ella *is* tall and blonde. And she *has* got long hair."

Carlos sounded confused.

Yes, thought Aubrey, but you might have asked yourself whether it was actually necessary to say so. Like that time when Molly had been unpacking the shopping and innocently told Jeremy that a man in the supermarket had offered to help her get some things down from the top shelves because she couldn't reach them. Jeremy had stopped what he was doing and looked exactly like Teddy had just now. When he asked what the man looked like, Molly had the good sense to say that she hadn't noticed.

"Do you think," Carlos continued, his tone doubtful, "that Teddy might have been, like, you know, jealous and that? Perhaps I should have lied," he mused. "Perhaps I should have said that Ella was a fat ugly wazzack with greasy hair and great big sweaty feet. But she isn't and it would feel, like, sort of wrong to say that. But it doesn't matter anyway, it's not as if I like her or anything. I mean, I like her as a friend and that, but that's all."

For several minutes Aubrey and Carlos sat silently when suddenly, releasing Aubrey from his grip, Carlos sprang from the bed and began spinning around in a strangely graceful dance. Aubrey watched him, his head on one side, as he fluttered his hands above his head and twirled around the room, making his T shirt ride up and his jeans slip down.

"If Teddy was jealous then that must mean that she really likes me. She must really care about me. Ha ha ha. Shove that up your posh bum, Sebastian."

Dancing across to the window sill and back again, he did a final twirl before sinking back down on the bed.

25

───────

IN THE SITTING room the lights on the Christmas tree twinkled in the flames from the fire. Aubrey had left Carlos upstairs trying to get Teddy back on WhatsApp and had come down to join Molly and Jeremy. Lying on the rug, he stretched his paws in front of him and gave a great sigh of contentment. Vincent, back home now and equally comfortable, lay draped across Jeremy's feet. In the background carol music played softly. Jeremy cradled his whisky glass and felt himself start to relax after an energetic afternoon on the golf course.

After talking to Dick on the phone this morning, he had felt the need to get out of the house, to get some air, to do something different to distract his thoughts. He'd decided on a round of golf, which he'd enjoyed because of, rather than in spite of, the weather. It had been the perfect solution. As he so often did, he blessed his father for introducing him to the game when he was a teenager, often turfing him out of bed on a Saturday morning to join him on the course. In fact, he was thinking about taking Carlos up to the club over the holiday period to see if he could capture his interest the way his father had done for him.

He sat back and looked at his wife, her head bent over a magazine, reading in the light from the little table lamp. He loved it when she got the Christmas music out. There was something about it all that made him feel safe and warm and sort of cosy. And right now, feeling safe and warm and sort of cosy was just what he needed. He hadn't told either Molly or Carlos yet about Annie although Molly knew that Dick had telephoned him. He'd fobbed her off with a vague story about setting meeting dates for the new year. She'd find out soon enough anyway, it would be all over the local papers in spite of Dick's best efforts to keep it quiet. But for now, this evening, he wanted to sit in peace and quiet.

"Any cards today?" he asked.

Molly looked up and nodded.

"Several. Including one from Clive and Rachel. They want to pay a visit in the new year."

Aubrey sat up straighter. He thought that they'd seen the last of the revolting couple. He had heard Jeremy describe them as the most sanctimonious, hypocritical people that he had ever had the misfortune to encounter. And Aubrey agreed, even though he didn't know what sanctimonious meant. Or hypocritical, come to that.

"Tell them we've moved to Australia," said Jeremy. "And are likely to remain there for some considerable time."

Molly laughed and then peered more closely at him.

"Are you all right?"

Jeremy nodded.

"I suppose so." He sipped at his whisky. "Everything just seems so surreal at the moment. I mean, all this business with Fireside House."

It was no good, he would have to tell her. He had never been able to keep anything from her. And he had never wanted to, really.

"When Dick phoned…" he paused and took another sip of his whisky.

Molly put the magazine down on the table.

"What about it? I thought that you were agreeing meeting dates."

"Well, yes. But there was something else." He breathed in deeply. "Annie, the tea lady, was found dead in the basement."

Molly's small fingers flew to her mouth.

"How dreadful. Was it… is it…"

Jeremy nodded.

"It looks very much like it."

He shifted Vincent from his feet and strode across to the window. He edged around the Christmas tree and pulled the curtain back slightly. How peaceful and silent everything looked when enveloped in snow. The road was empty of people and everybody was tucked up inside on this winter's night. In the bay windows of the houses opposite, the lights from the Christmas trees twinkled back at him. He pulled the curtain across again and turned to face Molly.

"First Adam and now Annie. If I was fanciful," he said, "I'd say that it's a bit like that Agatha Christie book. The one about the alphabet. The ABC murders."

"What happened in that?" asked Molly.

"The murderer went round killing people by their initials. So the first one was an A, the second one was a B and so on."

"But there've been two As" pointed out Molly, smiling. It was terrible news about the tea lady but at least if Jeremy was talking about his beloved Agatha he must be feeling a bit more cheerful. He had seemed so despondent when he went off to play golf that she had felt quite worried about him.

"True. Let's hope that the murderer isn't upping the ante and that there's not two people with the initial B at Fireside House." He paused and sipped at his whisky again, feeling the comforting warmth as it slipped down his throat. "But you know Molly, it all just seems so hard to believe. I mean why Annie of all people? Who on earth goes around killing tea ladies?"

From his comfortable place on the rug in front of the fire, Aubrey pondered the question. If it came to it, why did anybody ever kill anybody? But Jeremy was right. Why Annie in particular? It wasn't like she had anything much. He and Vincent had visited her little house with Eric a couple of times. Situated about a quarter of a mile from Fireside House along a small back lane, it was a modest two up, two down affair with very few luxury items apart from a rather large television situated in one corner of the sitting room. All in all, she was just an ordinary person. But, he suddenly recollected with a sinking feeling, there was one thing about her that you could say was a little less ordinary. One little habit she had that wasn't shared by the majority. She listened at doors. Was it possible that Annie might just have heard something that it wasn't was safe for her to know?

"Do you think that it's anything to do with Adam's death?" asked Molly.

"I think it must be," said Jeremy slowly. "It would be too much of a coincidence otherwise. But for the life of me I cannot see the connection. Two more different people you couldn't hope to meet."

"What do you know about Annie?" asked Molly.

"Not much," Jeremy admitted. "Only really that she was the tea lady and that she's worked at the Foundation forever. I only came across her once or twice. When I spoke to Dick he said that she lived on her own so he's got to find out about any relatives and so on. She did get on Dick's nerves though, I do know that."

"Why, what did she do?"

"I think, to use an old-fashioned term, Dick considered that she didn't know her place."

"In what way?"

"Well, at the last meeting that I was at, the one that they asked me to after Adam died, Annie just sort of strolled in with the coffee and started offering her opinions. Dick was quite sharp with her. He pretty much told her to mind her own business. Although," he added, "to be fair, given that she was an employee of the Foundation and also that she was at the lunch, it's as much her business as anybody else's."

Molly thought for a moment.

"I've known a few people like that. They don't usually mean any harm though. Often, they just haven't got enough in their own lives to keep them occupied, so they're a bit too interested in everybody else's. What's happening about her funeral?" she added.

"I'm not entirely sure. As I said, Dick needs to find out about any next of kin, but I think that if the Foundation can't find any, then they ought to make the arrangements themselves. I think that it's the least that they can do, given how long she worked there, and it's not like they can't afford it. And there'll be a good turn out as I assume that all the staff will attend."

"Will you go?"

"As the Chairman of Trustees I suspect that it's my duty."

They sat quietly for a moment. Funerals weren't exactly a barrel of laughs at the best of times but there was something even more poignant about a Christmas funeral.

26

MOLLY LEANED FORWARD and tipped another log on the fire. She watched for a moment as the log beneath it subsided and the flames reached up to embrace the new one. She felt suddenly very sad. How quickly people were forgotten. In ten years' time, maybe as few as five, who would remember Annie? Just a tea lady. Nobody of any significance. Until now that is. The manner of her death had catapulted her straight into the spotlight, so she was, after all, having her fifteen minutes of fame. Although not in a way that anybody would choose. So perhaps she would be remembered. If only as a footnote in a criminology reference book. She looked across at Jeremy.

"Does anybody know what Annie was doing in the basement?" she asked. "I mean, if her job was to make the tea why would she be down there?"

"One of the senior investigating officers plays golf at my club and he was there this afternoon…"

"I thought that you didn't like the old boys network?" interrupted Molly.

Jeremy looked sheepish.

"I don't." He grinned suddenly. "In theory. Anyway, don't tell me that there isn't an old girls network. I bet that there is."

"Might be."

Molly's dimples appeared making her look suddenly very young. Jeremy caught his breath. What would he do if he didn't have Molly? He felt a sudden protective rush sweep through him.

"Molly, you will be careful won't you? I mean, when you go out and so on."

Molly laughed.

"You'll be telling me not to open the door to strangers next."

"Yes, well, don't," Jeremy leaned forward, his tone earnest.

"Don't be silly. Anyway, what did your friend the police man say?"

Jeremy unhunched his shoulders and relaxed a little. He was being over-cautious and letting the Foundation business get to him, probably as a result of being so tired. The most recent Ofsted visit had been difficult and troubling and had left him feeling worried and anxious, not least for the pupils whom the school was clearly failing. The head, a small, pale depressed looking man, had seemed completely at his wits end as he explained to Jeremy the trouble that they had recruiting staff. At least a third of the current contingent were employed on a supply basis and, as Jeremy had discovered, were frequently not remotely qualified to teach the subjects that they had been given. He had discovered one of them in the staff room desperately photocopying pages from a text book to distribute to his next class.

He thought for a moment about his own experience of supply teachers. Like many permanent staff, he had been grateful when they could step in to fill a gap but other than that he had never really given them much thought. But, as he had now realised, they were often on the front line doing their best to paper over some very large cracks indeed. He had asked the teacher whom he had discovered photocopying the text book why he didn't apply for one of the many permanent vacancies at the school. The man had stopped his photocopying and simply looked at him. Because, he had said eventually, he had a wife with early on-set dementia. Because, he had said, he could only work on days when he could get somebody to act as carer for his wife. And because, he had said, a scheduled twenty minutes by the local authority was insufficient. After which he had simply sighed and gone back to his photocopying.

Jeremy leaned back and closed his eyes. It was as well that Christmas was nearly upon them. Some problems were too big for him to solve and he really could do with a break.

"This police officer," he continued eventually, opening his eyes again, "is called Dave. Nice bloke. Old school type copper."

"Is he supposed to be discussing cases with people?"

"Probably not," admitted Jeremy. "Anyway, we had a quick drink in the club house afterwards and he told me that the police aren't entirely sure where Annie was actually killed. They're looking at the possibility that she may not have been killed in the basement. That she may have been killed elsewhere and then taken down there. Although Dave doesn't think that's very likely."

Molly's brow crinkled.

"Why do they think that she might have been killed somewhere else?"

"Mostly because, as you said, there was no reason for her to be down in the basement in the first place. Nobody goes down there unless it's to find an old file, so if you're going to stash a body then it's as good a place as any. If it hadn't been for Lettie, poor old Annie could have been down there for goodness knows how long. Months, possibly."

"But," said Molly. "Surely that would have still been risky? Somebody would have gone down there eventually. Why not put her somewhere else?"

"Where though?" asked Jeremy. "If she was killed in Fireside House, then the only place to take her would be outside and then what would you do?"

Molly nodded.

"I see what you mean. You couldn't really go digging up the grounds and you wouldn't risk putting her in a car because of DNA and so on."

"Exactly," said Jeremy. "And even if the murderer did put her in a car, then where would he take her?"

"The sea?" suggested Molly, doubtfully. "The beach is only a short walk away."

Jeremy shook his head.

"Bodies have a propensity to get washed up again. And besides, there's always the danger of witnesses. Lots of people still walk on the beach, even when it's been snowing, and lugging bodies in and out of cars and across the sand isn't the work of a moment. And even if you managed it without being seen, you'd have to take it quite a long way out. You'd probably need a boat. And at this time of year, especially with the weather like it is…"

"I suppose so." Molly thought for a moment. "Could she possibly have been killed in her own home and then taken to the basement?"

"I don't think so. I've been thinking about that. If she was killed at home then, again, there would be the problem of witnesses. I mean, somebody might observe a visitor coming or going. And, as well as the possibility of DNA, there's still the problem of transporting the body around."

"The killer could just have left the body in her house," suggested Molly. "I mean, according to Dick she lived alone."

"True," Jeremy acknowledged. "But it would only be a

matter of time before somebody started looking for her. Like when she didn't turn up for work. And her home would be the first place to look. If she just didn't turn up then eventually one of the staff would have gone round to see if she was all right."

"The police are sure, are they, that she was actually killed? Deliberately, I mean."

"Completely," said Jeremy. "Dave told me that she had severe bruising to her face. It seems that she had been punched several times and then strangled."

Molly shuddered.

"The thing is," said Jeremy slowly, "I think whether or not Annie was killed in the basement, somebody employed at Fireside House must be implicated because who else would have had access? Any member of staff could go to the basement at any time so there's no reason why their DNA shouldn't be found there. And there's something else."

Jeremy paused and bit at his lower lip.

"She must have almost certainly been killed outside of office hours. Otherwise, how could she have been taken down to the basement without somebody noticing? If she had been left in the kitchen then somebody would have found her. Although Annie made the tea in the mornings and afternoons, lots of staff pop in and out of the kitchen to make themselves an extra cup. They keep their lunches in the fridge, too."

For a moment he fell silent, staring into the flames of the fire.

"But that then begs the question," he continued, "what was Annie doing in Fireside House after office hours? And if she wasn't in Fireside House after office hours, what was she doing in the basement?"

27

———

JEREMY ADJUSTED his black tie and looked in the mirror. Never one to pay too much attention to his personal appearance, even to his own eyes he looked rather drawn. He leaned in to his reflection and peered more closely. Molly had bought him some special vitamins but he wasn't sure that they were doing much good even though he had been taking them as instructed. Surely after two whole days he should have noticed a difference, especially as he had more or less given up drinking. Well, cut down anyway. A bit. He sighed and slipped on his jacket. Not too many days now till Christmas and a funeral to attend, and there was still Adam's to go although nobody had been told yet when that might be given that he had family spread right across the country. He had been half-hoping that the undertakers wouldn't have a space for Annie so that it could be put off until the new year but he had been out of luck. As the undertaker had explained to Harry, with a rather ghoulish relish, it was a warm spring that brought a full church yard, not a cold winter.

He felt a sudden rush of guilt. The whole thing would only take an hour or so and he shouldn't grudge it. After all, what was an hour? When he'd been teaching at Sir Frank's he had wasted hundreds of hours trying to teach English literature to groups of bored adolescents who had quite frequently looked at him as though he was mad. That was when they looked at him at all. Most of them had been glued to their phones, even though they were banned in classrooms. He had often thought that his pupils could have taught prison inmates a thing or two about smuggling in contraband. Anyway, as he had said to Molly, attendance at Annie's funeral was a duty and it was not one to be avoided, however much he might want to. Despite a thorough search, neither the police nor the Foundation had been able to come up with any next of kin, not even a distant cousin. Without him and the Foundation staff there would be nobody to say goodbye to the poor old girl. He hoped that when the time came and if it was necessary, somebody would do the same for him. He turned as Molly came in.

"How do I look? This jacket's a bit tight across the back."

"Fine. You look very smart." She crossed the room and brushed a speck of dust from his shoulder. "It's a long time since that black tie came out." She paused and looked into his tired eyes. "Are you sure that you don't want me to come with you?"

Jeremy shook his head.

"No. Honestly. There's no need. I'll be back before you know it."

Molly nodded.

"Are the Foundation laying on anything afterwards?"

"A few sandwiches and things, I think, back at Fireside House. The receptionist arranged it, nobody else seemed to have thought of it. She's a nice woman," he added. "Very thoughtful."

———

AT THE CREMATORIUM, the small group of mourners took up the first few rows. As at the Christmas lunch, the managers and the trustees sat at the front, each wearing a black tie and a suitably serious expression, and the office workers sat behind them. On the very last row, at the far end, sat Lettie, her hair tied neatly back with a black ribbon and her face pale in spite of the carefully applied make-up, which made her look even younger. From the corner of his eye, Jeremy studied her for a moment and wondered if this was her first funeral. Given her age, it probably was. Poor girl. From what he gathered, she had only just left school and her post at the Foundation was her first job. Whatever else her careers teacher might have prepared her for, the discovery of a dead body almost certainly wasn't on the list. And not just a dead body, but one that had very obviously been murdered. He would make a point of speaking to her afterwards, check that she was all right.

He turned round and then stood up along with everybody else as the small dark coffin was trundled in by the undertakers who then discreetly stood to one side as the service commenced. Jeremy stared for a moment at the wreath placed on top of the coffin. Clearly arranged and paid for by the Foundation, it consisted of an attractive glossy wreath of Christmas greenery and flowers. Whoever had chosen it, had chosen well. He felt his throat suddenly thicken. For all the talk of bodies and murders, they should all remember that Annie had been a real person with as much right to live as anybody else. She may have been irritating on occasion but so were lots of people. They didn't all end up alone, flung to the floor in a cold dark space with their life throttled out of them.

The tone of Dick's voice was sonorous, his words measured, as he extolled Annie's virtues to the little gathering. He praised her loyalty to the Foundation, her years of service, her reliability and her undoubted talent as a baker of delicious cakes. Jeremy watched, inwardly amused in spite of the solemnity of the occasion. You could almost believe that Dick had liked the woman. You had to give it to him though, he looked the part and he played it well. Standing there in his expensive beautifully cut dark suit and black tie, his crisp white shirt with the discreet gold cufflinks, he looked every inch the thing that he was not – an officer and a gentleman. Perhaps, he thought suddenly, that was Dick's real worth to the Foundation. He looked the part.

Dick attended, he knew, a number of formal events in his role as Chief Executive and with his upright appearance and neatly combed hair that even a strong wind didn't seem to disturb, he projected exactly the right image. As long as he didn't open his mouth too much and reveal what an intellectually challenged, self-centred bigot he was, people were taken in by him. Those same people would no doubt be astonished if they saw him in operation on a day to day basis. He had more in common with a Victorian work-house master than a modern senior manager. He would be astonished if Dick could even spell the word diversity, let alone implement it in the workplace.

He reigned his thoughts back in and listened harder as Dick continued.

"And of course, as many of us know, Annie did much to help local animals in distress, giving a great deal of her own time to help the poor unfortunate creatures…"

If Jeremy had to put money on it, he would swear that Dick hadn't written the eulogy himself. He doubted that Dick had even known that Annie helped with animal rescue. As far as Dick was concerned, Annie's only role in life was to bring him tea and coffee when he wanted it and to get out the dusters and vacuum cleaner when occasion demanded. It was, he thought, probably Harry who had actually penned the eulogy. He felt himself shiver slightly and made an effort to stand up straighter. Although the heating had been turned on in the building, it had clearly been done at the last minute and did very little to warm a room which had been designed to accommodate considerably more people than the sad little group bunched up together at the front. He let his mind wander and glanced across to the window. It had started snowing again.

28

———

BACK AT FIRESIDE HOUSE, the staff stood around the big committee table glad to be back in the warm. On the crisp white table cloth stood plates of shop-bought sandwiches cut into quarters and tiny sausage rolls stacked into neat golden pyramids. At the end of the table white paper plates and napkins stood ready for use. Ranged next to them on Annie's tea trolley were several pots of coffee and tea, with the Fireside House cups and saucers emblazoned with the charity's logo next to them. The receptionist, Jeremy thought, had done a good job. The whole thing looked entirely appropriate. Annie would have been pleased. He hoped that Dick had thought to thank her, although he doubted it. He would make a point of doing so himself before he left. He watched as the Chief Executive, without waiting to invite anyone else, reached across and helped himself to several prawn sandwiches and a sausage roll. Jeremy turned to the office staff who were standing about in small self-conscious clumps, clearly uncomfortable at being allowed access to a room that was normally only used by the managers.

"Do make a start," he said pleasantly, and handed a paper

plate and napkin to Lettie who was standing nearest to him. She glanced nervously around and then gingerly picked a single sandwich from the nearest plate. Her hand hovered over it for a moment.

"Thank you, Mr Goodman. Sir," she added.

Jeremy smiled.

"I haven't been knighted yet. Mr Goodman is fine. Or Jeremy, if you prefer."

Lettie looked up at him and then over at Dick who was now helping himself to a second round of sandwiches. She giggled suddenly, a small trickling sound that was barely audible but suddenly reminded Jeremy of a girl called Sophie whom he had taught in his last year at Sir Frank's. A small, nervous girl from what was euphemistically described as an unfortunate background, she barely spoke up in class. Nevertheless, she had turned out to have rather more about her than outward appearances would suggest. Resisting the urge to lounge about picking her nose with most of the rest of the class, she had determinedly worked hard, fought off the bullies when occasion demanded, and had been one of the few achievers of five or more GCSE's in the history of the school. The last he had heard she had gained a place at Cambridge. He studied Lettie a little more closely.

"So, Lettie, isn't it?" he asked.

The girl nodded and began to cautiously nibble at her sandwich.

"Is this your first job, Lettie?"

Lettie nodded again.

"And have you settled in all right? Are you enjoying it?"

Lettie put her sandwich down.

"Yes, everybody is very nice," she said politely.

Jeremy resisted the temptation to ask her what she wanted to be when she grew up, and ploughed on.

"Lettie," he hesitated, and then continued because he was

about as sure as he could be that none of the managers had said it. "I'm so sorry that you were the one to find Annie. It must have been dreadful for you."

"I've never seen a dead body before. Except on the television," she added.

Jeremy wished that he could say the same. The last bodies that he had seen had been murder victims and he was unlikely to forget any of them.

"I've never been to a funeral before, either."

Jeremy looked at her, his eyes full of sympathy. Good God. What an introduction to the real world. He hadn't seen Annie's body but Dave had given him a pretty graphic description. The shock for the girl must have been awful. He wondered suddenly if anybody had suggested that she take a few days off after it happened, that she might even need some kind of counselling. He would bet that nobody had. He was about to suggest it himself and then stopped. Dick could be very prickly if he thought that his authority had been usurped and the management of the Foundation staff was very clearly his responsibility. He was already outraged at the recent turn of events, with the result that everybody had suffered. Now would not be a good time to annoy him even more.

"Well, you must try to put it out of your mind," Jeremy said gently. "I know it's not easy but try to look ahead. It will be Christmas soon. I expect that you've got lots of parties to go to and so on, haven't you?"

Lettie continued as though he hadn't spoken. Having been initially reluctant to speak, now the words tumbled out.

"I didn't recognise her at first. It didn't look like Annie. Her face was sort of all different colours and it looked as though she wasn't real. Like a kind of dummy, you know, like they have in shop windows. And then I noticed her overall. She always wore it. It was torn," she added.

Jeremy fell silent. If the girl needed to talk, it was probably better to let her.

"The police asked me lots of questions. Like whether I touched her or anything." Her eyes stared at him, filled with horror at the very thought. "I said that I didn't. They said what was she doing down there and I said that I didn't know."

In spite of his determination to let the girl speak, Jeremy couldn't resist it.

"So she wouldn't normally go down there for anything?"

"No, I don't think so." Lettie shook her head. "Nobody really likes going to the basement, it's a bit sort of spooky. Some of the Foundation china and stuff was stored down there so I suppose that sometimes Annie might have fetched some up if there was some kind of event on, like the garden party. One of the previous Chief Executives had it designed for the centenary; it's got the Foundation logo on it in gold." She nodded towards the cups and saucers stacked on Annie's tea trolley. "There's loads of it. Dinner plates and everything. It has to be hand-washed. It can't go in the dishwasher."

Jeremy stared at her. What had she just said that had jogged something in his brain?

29

JEREMY UNPEELED the shred of Sellotape that was sticking to his wrist and surveyed the mess of festive wrapping paper in front of him. Molly and Carlos had gone to the carol concert at the college and, suffering from an incipient sore throat, he had decided to take the opportunity to sit by the fire and wrap their Christmas presents while they were out. The trouble was that he had never got the hang of this present-wrapping lark. Anything that he wrapped always ended up looking like something that the bomb squad had been having a go at. Molly, on the other hand, always wrapped presents beautifully, often with little ribbons and bows and things attached. She was good at sewing on buttons, too. He'd tried it himself a couple of times but he just couldn't manage the needle, it was too small. But when it came to presents, even Carlos usually made a better fist of gift wrapping than he did. Bags, he thought. That was the answer. Those little gift bag things. Even he could manage to stuff a present in one of those. He'd go out in the morning and get some. He sat back and gave a virtuous sigh. Not only would it make an impossible task easy, he'd be saving the planet too because the bags could be used again.

Under the Christmas tree, Aubrey sat watching the baubles reflecting the room in which they were sitting. Carlos had told him that when he was small his mother had said that Christmas baubles had little people living in them and, looking at them now, Aubrey could half convince himself of the truth of it. He thought for a moment about Carlos's mother. Small, loud, quite definitely mad and with a voice that could induce sonic shock at twenty paces, she had cared with all her heart and soul for Carlos. Of that there could be no doubt. Everything that she had ever done had been for him and he knew how much Carlos still missed her. On the window sill, his tail hanging below the closed curtains, Vincent sat watching the snow.

Jeremy reached into the carrier bag next to him and pulled out a large bottle of the cologne that he'd bought. It was the same one that Molly always bought for him and to which Carlos occasionally helped himself. Well, he'd have his own now and it would go very nicely into a little gift bag. He put it to one side while he tumbled out onto the carpet the rest of the presents that he had bought. He studied them for a moment. He was particularly pleased with the small bowl that he had bought for Molly. He had seen it in the window of an antique shop in town and immediately been attracted by it. It had a ruby and silver prettiness that he knew Molly would like. The owner of the shop had thought that it was made at the beginning of the last century, much the same age as their house. He picked it up and turned it over in his hands. It had a lovely feel to it. Perhaps he would buy some hyacinth or crocus bulbs to go in it.

He turned his head at the sound of the front door opening. Gathering up the gifts and sheets of wrapping paper that were spread in front of him he shoved them hastily back into the carrier bag.

"You two are back early. I thought that you'd be ages yet."

"They played it fast," said Carlos, grinning.

"They finished early because of the weather," Molly explained. "It's practically blizzard conditions out there now. How's your throat?"

She moved towards the fire and began rubbing her hands together.

"Sore," said Jeremy. "But nothing that a large whisky won't cure." He turned to Carlos, suddenly curious. "How did you celebrate Christmas in Brazil?" he asked. "Was it exciting?"

Carlos nodded, his face animated.

"Yeah, it was really good. Even Dad used to join in. He used to pretend to be Papai Noel. Father Christmas," he added. "I always knew it was him though. I could smell the drink on him. Mum used to say that he should be called Papai Whisky. And where we lived, in Sao Paulo, they used to have big firework displays and everybody was happy and there was dancing and stuff. It was all a bit different when we came here."

He fell silent for a moment, remembering the first Christmas night that he and his mother had spent in the dismal little cold flat in the Meadows. There had been no firework displays, no dancing and singing. Outside was thick darkness, the street lights having been smashed by vandals again. The only sound of merriment came from the drunks meandering their way home after spending what little they had in the local pub, a squat, modern, over-lit building that belied its name of The Jolly Farmer. It had been years since there were any farmers within ten miles of the place, let alone a jolly one. He had sat closer to his mother and turned the radio up, knowing that it wouldn't be too long before the sound of shouting and screaming from one or more of the flats around them echoed through the block. If it was particularly spectacular, the police cars would arrive shortly after.

They had known nobody and it had been just the two of

them, huddled on the sofa and listening to carols on the radio. In those early days, they hadn't even had a television. Living on the income from the cash in hand cleaning jobs that Maria had managed to obtain in a couple of shops and a local factory, they hadn't dared to try to claim any benefits. As immigrants who were not only in the country illegally but were also unlawfully occupying a council flat which the tenant had sub-let contrary to the terms of his lease, their main priority had been to stay well under the radar. Maria's fear and distrust of officialdom was not without foundation. Her words, drummed into him, reverberated even now.

"Carlos, you must not speak to the people who ask questions and do the nose poke. Often they will have the board clip. And a pen," she added as an afterthought. "If they ask you where you have come from you must say nothing. For if they know that we are from Brazil, they will depart us. It is definite. We will be departed."

And, as Carlos now realised, she hadn't been wrong. Even when she had enrolled him at Sir Frank's she had given only his name and address and ignored any requests for further information. It had been difficult but she had done her best in the ways she knew how. And saying nothing was one of those ways. But it wasn't as though they were criminals. Not really. Not in the true sense. They didn't deal drugs or steal things. They didn't carry knives or threaten people. Their only reason for being in England was to try to make a better life for themselves. Maria had been more than prepared to work hard and grasp any opportunity that came their way, desperate to flee from rat-infested rooms and abject poverty and to give her only son a better chance than she had ever had. She would have done anything to get them away from the squalor that they had both been born into. But the authorities, Carlos knew, even at that age, wouldn't see it like that. Not for the first time, he wondered what his status was now. Was he still an illegal immigrant? It was a question that he had never quite dared to ask Molly and Jeremy but he knew that he would have to face it at some point.

But Maria had tried her very best that first Christmas, as she always did. There had been home-made paper chains, cut from coloured paper that Carlos had filched from the art room at school, and a small roast chicken for dinner that she had bought cheaply from the butcher just as he was closing on Christmas Eve. She had given him a pair of jeans that she had bought from a stall on the market and a woolly jumper that he suspected she had bought from a charity shop. It was made from cheap wool and far too big, but she had assured him that he would grow into it. It was warm and cosy and he still had it. And he still wore it on cold winter mornings. He had given her a home-made card, some cheap perfume and some artificial flowers that he had bought from the bargain shop in town. In all the time that they had lived in the Meadows, right up until the time that Maria was murdered, the flowers had stood in a little jug in the hall. They were the only bright thing in the flat.

Carlos looked across at Molly and Jeremy. They were watching him anxiously. He smiled.

"This is really good as well," he said, waving his hand vaguely around the room and reaching down to stroke Aubrey. "This is great."

30

Jeremy felt a great choking rage billow up in his throat and his heart raced as he reached for the figure clutching the bowl that he had bought for Molly. The sweat streamed down his face as he tried to grab it from behind and pull it towards him. The figure slipped away from him and he found himself crunching across their best dinner service which was smashed and strewn in pieces across the floor. He staggered and fell, falling forwards on his knees, his hands flailing upwards. Gasping for air he struggled upright and opened his eyes. He lay still for a moment, confused. Slowly, he felt his heart rate steady as his eyes became accustomed to the darkness. In the distance he could hear the sound of a solitary goods train chugging its way through the night. It took him immediately back to when he was a child, staying with his grandmother and being put to bed in the bedroom that had been his father's. The red-bricked terraced house had been not too far from the railway station and every time that a train went through, the sash windows rattled. A comforting sound that told him all was right in his little world. He turned his head. The bedside clock showed three am.

The dark shape by the door moved towards the bed. Glancing across to check that Molly was still asleep, Jeremy relaxed back against the pillow. He dropped his hand down and stroked Aubrey's back.

"Hello, old mate," he whispered. "What are you doing in here?"

Looking after you, thought Aubrey. Restless, unable to sleep and bored without Vincent who was snoring in his basket and recovering from wherever he had been earlier in the day, he had wandered upstairs and put his nose round the bedroom door. Whatever was going on with Jeremy clearly wasn't good. Twisting and turning, his legs getting wrapped up in the sheets, Jeremy had clearly been in distress and for several moments he had stood in the doorway, uncertain what to do. In the end he had simply padded across the room while he thought about it.

Jeremy slid his legs out of bed, unhooked his dressing gown from the back of the bedroom door, and made his way towards the landing. Aubrey followed him.

Tiptoeing down the stairs and into the kitchen, Jeremy switched on the kettle and stared out of the window. The snow had settled, covering everything in a soft white blanket that gave a romantic glow at this hour in the morning. It looked inviting, and almost warm, but it would be, he knew, bitterly cold out there. Pity any poor creature out on the streets tonight. Clutching the hot mug of tea, he made his way back upstairs and into his study. Switching on the desk lamp and settling Aubrey on his lap, Jeremy stared for a moment at the blank screen of his computer. He shivered slightly. That had been such an odd dream. Normally, he didn't dream at all. Or if he did, he remembered it only briefly on waking until it shimmered and broke into a thousand pieces before disappearing. But this dream was different, this dream was staying with him. He could see it in every detail; he could feel the jagged edges of the dinner service as he stumbled across it, the tangle of panic and fear that had knotted itself in his chest. But for the life of him he couldn't think why on earth their dinner service had featured.

Bought in an antique shop not long after they were married, the dinner service was kept for best. Keeping things for best wasn't a practice that he usually approved of, mainly because it was something that his mother often did, with the result that she rarely got to use or appreciate some of the lovely things that she had acquired over the years. But somehow, with the dinner service, and perhaps because it had cost more than they could really afford even though the antique shop owner had reduced the price for them on the basis that it wasn't quite complete, it had seemed fitting that it should only be brought out on high days and holidays. Fine china, with a delicate understated pattern of honeysuckle and roses, the last time it had been used was when Molly had cooked a special dinner to celebrate Carlos's exam results. But that was ages ago, in the summer, so why should he be thinking of it now?

Draining his tea, he propped his elbows on his desk and rested his cheeks on his fists. Slowly, a memory began to filter into his brain. Somebody had been talking about dinner services. Who had it been? Unbidden, an image of Lettie began to appear at the forefront of his mind like a pixilated picture slowly forming, her small child-like face staring innocently up at him. Of course, it had been Lettie. She had been talking about the Foundation's special dinner service, the white china with the gold logo. A prickle of excitement ran through him. Lettie had said that most of the dinner service had been stored in the basement. And of course... that was what Annie was doing down there. She hadn't been down there looking for any files or anything improbable like that, she had been collecting the dinner service. But no, that couldn't be right. Lettie had said that the dinner service was only used for special occasions, like the annual garden party, and as far as he was aware, there had been no special occasions of late.

Shifting in his chair, he leaned back and ran his hand over Aubrey's head. There was something just outside of his grasp, something important. He thought harder about his dream. It hadn't just been their special dinner service, the Christmas present that he had bought Molly, the bowl, that had been in the dream too. So what was it about the bowl and their dinner service? He reached down into the carrier bag containing the gifts that he had bought and which he'd stored up here earlier, away from prying eyes. He pulled out the bowl. Placing it carefully on his desk, he gently turned it round and studied it. It was small. It was pretty. There was something about the warm ruby colour that was stirring a memory but he couldn't think what for the moment. So what else was there about it? He suddenly sat up straight. Of course, it was an antique. And so was the claret jug used for the Founder's toast. What was more likely than that the claret jug was stored down in the basement with the dinner service? And if so, was that what Annie was doing down there? Adam had told him that she was responsible for washing it and getting it to the hotel so had she also been responsible for taking it back to Fireside House? At that stage there had been no suspicion that Adam's collapse was attributable to anything but natural causes. There was no reason why Annie shouldn't have simply taken the jug home with her and returned it when she had cleaned and polished it.

Jeremy stared ahead of him, his thoughts racing. If what he surmised was correct, and Annie had been replacing the claret jug in the basement, then her murderer must have either followed her or had been waiting for her down there. He hesitated. That last couldn't be right. The murderer wouldn't know when, or even if, she would go to the basement and he wouldn't just be waiting on the off-chance. He could have been left hanging around there all day. So, he, or she, he supposed, must have followed her. But why then would the mere act of Annie putting the jug away result in the violence that followed? He put his head in his hands and pushed his palms against his eye sockets. He needed to think logically. He needed, as Poirot would have said, to use his little grey cells. He raised his head again, pulled a pad of paper towards him and wrote rapidly.

31

———

WHO? What? Where? When? Why? Jeremy stared at the five words with satisfaction. Somehow the mere act of putting something down on paper felt like progress. The questions looked stark on the page but he was off to a good start. He already knew the answer to three of them. It was the Who and the Why that were the posers. What he needed to do was clear his mind and think logically. Perhaps he should build little card houses. That was what Poirot did, he knew. He and Molly did have some packs of cards, he was sure of it. The last time they'd used them had been when they'd had a power cut and they had all played rummy by candle light. But that was ages ago and he had no idea where the cards were now. By the time he found them he would have wakened the whole house. Anyway, he'd never built a card house before, he didn't know how to do it.

Forget card houses, that was just a distraction. What he needed to do was to focus and concentrate on the two unanswered questions. Whatever way he looked it at, it was fairly obvious that Annie and Adam's murders must be linked somehow. It was, surely, beyond the realms of coincidence that there could have been two murderers roaming around at more or less the same time. It reminded him of the story about the hitchhiker who got in the car and then said, how do you know that I'm not a psychopath? To which the driver replied, what are the chances of there being two psychopaths in the same car? It was story which had always amused him but, be that as it may, the odds were roughly the same in this situation. The town was a medium-sized, rather sedate, place. The chances of two murders happening at all, never mind both being connected to the Foundation, were remote to say the least.

He tapped his pen on his desk top. They were such different types of murder, not only the method but the victims themselves were almost total opposites. If the murderer had some kind of modus operandi, it wasn't revealing itself. He doodled on the pad while he thought about it, long open swirls that pretty much reflected the pattern of his thoughts. If Adam had been poisoned, and it seemed fairly certain that he had, it would have required a certain amount of planning and nerve but no actual physical strength, whereas the attack on Annie had been one of brute force. There had been no subtlety about it. He reflected, not for the first time, that whoever had followed Annie down to the basement must have had a legitimate reason not only to go down there but to be in Fireside House at all. Which meant that it was almost certainly a member of staff. He thought about the women in the office. They seemed such nice ordinary women. What reason would any of them have to kill Annie? But, on the other hand, people did harbour dark secrets and he knew, as did everyone else, that Annie listened at doors. But if one of the women had killed Annie, why had they killed Adam? Equally, if one of them had killed Adam, why then kill Annie? What was the connection?

He thought for a moment about Annie, conjuring up an image of her in his mind. Rather small, not particularly overweight but stocky in build. Quite elderly but definitely not feeble. She was what his grandmother would have called solid. His impression of her had been that she was more than capable of giving as good as she got. And then some. Given her truculent attitude at the best of times, he was certain that she would have fought back or tried to escape. In fact, that had been borne out by the evidence that her apron had been torn, but clearly she had been overwhelmed. Why hadn't she screamed or shouted? Surely the receptionist would have heard her? Fireside House was generally very quiet, there would be no other sounds to drown her out. And the heavy door to the basement was just around the corner from the receptionist's desk and it always stood open. Perhaps, he thought with a shudder, she hadn't had time. If she had been attacked from behind...

He recalled Annie's words when she had strolled into the management meeting with her tea trolley after Adam had died. She had said something to the effect that the police were bound to ask questions. That, in her opinion, somebody knew more than they were letting on. He thought that it was unlikely, given that she did the rounds of the whole of Fireside House dispensing tea and coffee, she had resisted the urge to share her thoughts with everybody else, in spite of Dick's instruction. But had she really known something? Or was she just trying to make herself seem important? Whichever it was, it seemed likely that somebody had thought the former. Or, in any event, wasn't taking any chances. And so, logically, that must mean that Annie's death was connected to Adam's murder. His mind veered off towards Adam's murder again.

He laid his pen down and tried to organise his thoughts. If the poison had been placed in the claret jug, then it must have been an employee of the Foundation. They were the only people that would know that the Chairman of the trustees drank from it, and nobody else. Which meant that the murderer had thought it through, taken the poison with them and then waited the chance to slip it into the waiting claret jug. And that chance had very conveniently come when they all had a break before the toast. There had been people milling about, nipping in and out to the cloakrooms, making calls on their mobiles. It could have been any one of them. But would that work? What if there hadn't been an opportunity to slip through to the kitchen? And if there had, what if there had been kitchen staff in there? But the point was, that there had been an opportunity. And there had been nobody in the kitchen. He realised even as the thoughts formed, that in a sense it didn't matter. Whoever had committed this terrible act, clearly had nerves of steel. If the coast hadn't been clear on that day, he, or she, would simply have waited for another opportunity.

He picked up his pen again and pulled his pad of paper towards him. The headings that he had scribbled down stared back at him. As far as Annie was concerned, the answer to 'why' was probably that in pursuing her favourite pastime of listening at doors, Annie had heard something. Or at least somebody thought that she did. But what was it that the murderer thought that Annie had heard? What secrets had been discussed at Fireside House that her listening ear had picked up? Or, perhaps she had seen something at the Christmas lunch. Annie wasn't stupid. She might not have realised the significance of what she had seen at first but had put two and two together later. He pressed his lips more tightly together and turned to the 'who' question, trying to picture in his mind the attack on Annie as it might have happened. Annie bustling her way down the basement steps, busying herself replacing the claret jug. A silent figure creeping up on her from behind. Perhaps her killer had clamped a hand over her mouth which would explain why she didn't scream. And then, as she struggled to get away, tearing her overall in the process.

Perhaps he had hit her before fastening his hands around her throat.

But whoever it was had been taking a huge risk. While he might have been lucky in slipping down to the basement unseen, what if one of the office staff had seen him coming back up? The ladies cloakroom door was opposite the basement and one of the office staff could have easily run into him in the corridor there. If the attacker was a man, and he thought that it was, then there were only four men employed at Fireside House and none of them had any reason to be down in the basement. If they had wanted something they would have rung down to the main office and asked for someone to bring it up. If one of the office workers had seen any of the managers emerging from the basement, then given what had happened, surely she would have remembered and mentioned it.

He reached out to stroke Aubrey, who was by now laying stretched out across his desk and regarding him solemnly with his beautiful green gold eyes. Aubrey rolled onto his side and exhaled a sigh of contentment. He liked being in Jeremy's study, there was something really cosy about it, although what they were doing in there in the middle of the night, he had no idea. But it was better than being downstairs, bored, waiting for Vincent to wake up. He pricked his ears as Jeremy spoke, his voice low and thoughtful.

"The thing is Aubrey, it must have been one of the managers. I mean, it just has to be. But not Dick," he added. Aubrey agreed. From the little that he had seen of Dick, while he might have cheerfully fastened his hands around Annie's throat, he certainly didn't have the intelligence or planning capability to carry out Adam's murder. Aubrey had sneaked into his office a few days ago, just out of curiosity. The man had been playing some kind of picture game on his tablet, which he quickly thrust aside, sitting up straighter and assuming a grave expression as his secretary came in with some letters for him to sign. Letters which the other three managers had drafted.

"So we're agreed, are we?" said Jeremy. "Not Dick."

Aubrey let out a small purr in appreciation. Agreed.

"But," continued Jeremy, "isn't that what they always do in detective books? Isn't it always the least likely person?" He smiled suddenly. "On that basis then it was certain to have been Lettie. Applying the old rule of whoever sees the dead body first is often the last person to see it alive, it has to be."

Not Lettie, thought Aubrey. He had been watching with Vincent while Yvette comforted her in the hall. The girl had been genuinely shocked and upset. There was no way that she could have faked it. Anyway, if it was her, why raise the alarm? Why not just leave Annie down there? It was almost certainly the last place that anybody would have thought of looking for her. Also, Lettie was slight, bordering on the frail. Aubrey had seen Annie trundling her laden tea trolley around and lifting the big metal teapot with ease. She would have made mincemeat of Lettie, advanced years notwithstanding.

"So you see, Aubrey, I think that really, all things considered, it has to be Max, Nigel or Harry."

For some reason, a song that Jeremy's mother used to sing to him when he was little danced into his mind. Bill and Ben, Bill and Ben, which of those two flowerpot men, was it Bill or was it Ben? He hadn't had a clue who these flowerpot men were but he remembered that he had liked the sound of it, especially sung in his mother's light musical voice. There had been something about some kind of weed thing, too. He smiled at the memory. But his three suspects weren't flowerpot men. They were real big grown-up people, one of whom may have done some terrible things.

32

———

HE LOOKED up as the study door opened and Carlos's tousled head appeared. He yawned and rubbed his eyes.

"I woke up and saw the light under the door. What are you two doing?"

Jeremy grinned at him.

"Playing detectives."

Carlos crossed the room and stroked Aubrey and then sat in the small armchair, wrapping his dressing gown, an old one of Jeremy's that he had taken a fancy to, more tightly around him. Jeremy looked at him. When Carlos had first started wearing the dressing gown it had grazed his ankles. Now it barely came below his knees.

"What are you detecting? Is it about the stuff that's been going on at Fireside House?"

Jeremy nodded, amused as always at the teenage capacity for acceptance. Far from being surprised that Jeremy was up at three in the morning talking to Aubrey and apparently detecting, it clearly seemed perfectly normal to him. What, he wondered, would Carlos have said if he had told him that they were perfecting a thermo nuclear device with which they planned to take over the world. Carlos would probably just have nodded and asked how it was going.

"I was just trying to work out what happened," he said. "I woke up and couldn't go back to sleep so I started sifting through what I know. And what I think I know," he added.

For a moment, Carlos fell silent. He had been more upset at the news about Annie's death than Adam's and Jeremy thought that he knew why even though Carlos hadn't known either of them. To Carlos, Adam was some posh bloke in a suit who worked for a bank. But Annie, from what Jeremy had told him, had been like his mother. Older, but a similar type. Just an ordinary woman, the kind that nobody much notices until something isn't done, like an office cleaned or afternoon tea served. They were noticed only for what they didn't do, never for anything that they did do. They were the kind of women that didn't count other than in their capacity of making other peoples' lives easier and more comfortable. And both of them had their lives taken from them for somebody else's convenience.

"I forgot to tell you earlier," said Carlos at last. "There was somebody in the kitchen at that Mistletoe hotel place. Ella told me."

Jeremy stared at him while he attempted to unpack what Carlos had just said.

"When you say that somebody was in the kitchen?"

"Somebody who shouldn't have been there."

"Right."

Jeremy looked thoughtful. Never mind who Ella was, that could wait.

"You mean on the day that Adam was poisoned?"

Carlos nodded and yawned again.

"And Ella was at the hotel? In the kitchen?"

"She works there. She was on shift that day."

"And did Ella tell you anything about this person?"

"It was a man. In a suit," he added.

"Did she tell you anything else?"

"No. She only saw his back. He was going out of the fire door. She said that at the time she thought it was the manager but it wasn't. This bloke was taller. Anyway, when you think about it, why would the manager be going out of the fire door?"

Jeremy sat back and thought about what Carlos had just said. Why indeed? If the stranger in the kitchen wasn't the manager and wasn't a chef or waitress, who in any event would have been wearing whites or the black uniform of the waitresses, then he was probably a guest. The hotel only had one dining room and that had been deployed to the Fireside Foundation that lunchtime. And the only men wearing suits at the lunch were the managers. And, he suddenly realised with a sinking heart, all of the trustees including himself. But, he thought, brightening again, none of the trustees had been at Fireside House when Annie was killed. Which brought him back to the four managers again.

Why do you think that Adam bloke was killed?" asked Carlos. "I mean, like, did he have enemies and that?"

"I really don't know," Jeremy admitted. "I don't think so. I've been trying to think about what I know about him. I know, for instance, that he was very different from the previous Chair of Trustees. From what I gathered, the last Chair just used to turn up at meetings, sign whatever he was asked to sign and claim his expenses. Adam thought that the Chairman of Trustees should take a more active role. He wanted to shake things up a bit."

"Maybe," said Carlos, "somebody didn't want to be shaken up."

33

———

AUBREY WAITED until Vincent had finished picking at the food in his bowl. He had eventually woken up just before daybreak, clearly still tired. Aubrey nodded towards the garden.

"Coming out for some fresh air?"

The snowman that Carlos had built was still standing strong, a fat robin perched on its carrot nose and pecking at it. The two cats paused and regarded the bird for a moment while it stared boldly back at them with beady little black eyes.

"This snow bloke," said Vincent. "Still don't get it, mate."

"Me neither," said Aubrey. And they strolled on.

"Fancy a visit to see how Eric's doing?" asked Vincent.

"Could do," said Aubrey.

Together, they ran lightly across the lawn and towards the road leading into town.

———

FROM THE SECOND FLOOR WINDOW, Nigel watched the cats as they walked across to the shrubbery and came to a halt by the holly tree. What was the collective noun for a group of cats, he wondered? It ought to be something like a sinister. They always looked like they were plotting something. As he watched, the three of them turned their heads and stared up at him. It was oddly disconcerting. Refusing to be intimidated by a gang of cats, he pushed open the window and stuck his head out. The snow had stopped falling now and the air smelt fresh and clean. Perhaps he'd take a walk in a bit. He could do with some fresh air and his desk was clear, ready for the Christmas break as per Dick's orders.

He glanced across the grounds. The fallen snow added a festive prettiness to the scene, making it look like the front of a traditional Christmas card. All it needed was a couple of rosy-cheeked children and a lady in a Victorian dress, hands encased within a fur muff, to complete the scene. He smiled and let his mind wander away in the direction of canals and narrow boats. He half-closed his eyes as his thoughts drifted along with the boat and he started to lose himself in his daydream. He could feel the gentle thrum of the engine as he steered his way competently towards the next lock. Ava was at his side, her face tilted up to him, wine glass in hand. She looked happy and relaxed, just as he intended that she should be. The smell of fresh bread that they had bought at the last village bakery wafted upwards from the galley kitchen, his skin felt warm from the gentle sun... his mouth suddenly tightened. Nothing and nobody was going to stop him having his dream. He had been through the accounts and investments again last night. There was more than enough to get him what he wanted. He would ride out this storm. Henry Holdings was lying dormant. They had agreed that there would be no more purchases. In due course, when all this fuss had died down, they would quietly wind it up. And that would be that. Farewell Henry Holdings.

He turned round as a light tap sounded on the door and Lettie tiptoed in carrying a large tray. Just outside of the door he could see the outline of one of the other women, presumably there to make sure that Lettie didn't make a mess of things but also because, as he had noticed, since Annie's murder, none of the women ever went anywhere within the building on their own now. He envied them in a way. The office staff seemed to be able to bond together, to support each other, in a way that the managers had never been able to. Or, if he was honest, ever tried to.

He watched as Lettie stood hesitating for a moment, her small hands clutching the tray as though she was afraid of dropping it. As the youngest, and newest, member of staff, Dick had given Lettie the job of making the tea until a replacement for Annie could be found. The fact that it might not have been the most sensitive thing to do, given that Lettie had discovered Annie's body, seemed not to have occurred to him. But then, like many intellectually challenged people, Dick had the hide of a rhinoceros. The girl smiled nervously at him. He smiled back while he tried to remember her name. Was it Lottie? Without speaking, Lettie carefully placed the tray on his desk and removed a blue china cup and saucer and a plate with two biscuits. She tucked the tray back under her arm and bit her bottom lip. Her big blue eyes blinked, her expression wary.

"Is that all right? Sir," she added.

"Lovely. Thank you, Lottie." Nigel sat back down at his desk and sipped at his tea. He doubted that she'd ever been up on to this floor before. Apart from Annie delivering tea and coffee, only the cleaners, Dick's secretary, and one or two of the longer serving members of the office staff ventured up here, and that was only to deliver files or take orders. He watched as Lettie backed out of the room, clearly relieved that she had accomplished her task without a mishap. In the office next door he could hear Dick talking.

He listened, half amused, as the sound of Dick's voice

filtered through. Dick was assuming the voice that he always did when speaking on the telephone. It sounded like a cross between a pre-war British army officer and somebody mimicking a minor member of the royal family. He sipped at his tea and sighed. He had definitely drawn the short straw in having his office next to Dick's. Max and Henry were on the opposite side of the landing and thus were spared the sound of Dick playing at being the Chief Executive. The man even adopted the same tone when talking to the local pest control operative, a small insignificant man with an unfortunate resemblance to the poor little creatures that he routinely slaughtered. However, whoever it was that Dick was speaking to now was clearly not going to be fobbed off.

He bit into one of his biscuits and listened harder.

"The staff are rather busy at the moment, you know." Nigel smiled. Dick's voice had risen slightly in register. He must be getting riled. "It's a dreadful rush to get everything ready for the Christmas break."

Nigel snorted. Nothing at the Foundation was ever a dreadful rush, and certainly not in Dick's office. He wondered, for the millionth time, what on earth Dick did all day. Nothing productive, that was for sure.

"And," Dick continued, "I really don't think that we can have any more disruption. The staff have been very upset with all the comings and goings lately."

Nigel grimaced and picked up his second biscuit. Only Dick could describe two murders as 'comings and goings'. Well, no matter how hard Dick tried to distance himself and the Foundation from the 'comings and goings' as he called it, the police hadn't finished with them yet. Dick was just going to have to weather it like everybody else.

34

JEREMY TURNED up the collar of his overcoat and crunched his way through the snow towards the small department store. He was glad that he had walked. Apart from the fact that it would be difficult to drive in this weather, after being up half the night he felt the need to shake himself up a bit. It had been gone five o'clock before he had finally gone back to bed and even then he had slept only fitfully. Carlos, with all the resilience of youth, had been his usual bright-eyed self at the breakfast table, in spite of having spent the early hours talking to Jeremy in his study. In contrast, Jeremy felt sluggish and scratchy. It reminded him of those long hours spent on revision before his finals. But unlike then, it would take more than a cat nap and a pint of lager to get him going again.

He hunched his shoulders as he felt the light chill of the wind whip across his face, bringing with it a fresh flurry of light snow. Pausing before the brightly lit window of the local bookstore, he stared in. There were several books on display that had been on his wanted list for ages. He hesitated and then ploughed on. He needed to focus on the task in hand. What did you buy as presents for an assorted group of ten or so women of varying ages and situations about whom, in truth, he knew very little? He should, he thought ruefully, have thought this one through a bit more. At the very least, he should have consulted with Molly before setting out. She would almost certainly have had a better idea of what to buy than he did.

He had rung Dick this morning on an impulse. He very much wanted to talk to the staff, preferably without any of the managers being present, and to arrive bearing gifts was as good a way in as any. After all, they had all been present at the Christmas lunch and they had all been employed at Fireside House when Annie was murdered. One of them just might say something that would set him on the right path. The idea of giving them each a little Christmas gift to thank them for their work this year would provide the perfect opportunity. The problem was that he really didn't know anything about them as individuals. He had absolutely no idea what any of them might like. He could always buy gift cards, he supposed. Those general ones that you could spend anywhere.

He rejected the idea of gift cards almost immediately. They were too impersonal. Also, if he spent too much it looked like showing off and if he spent too little it looked mean. Chocolates? Wine? No, wine wouldn't do. Lettie was certainly under age and one or two of the others might be too. While he might turn a blind eye to Carlos necking the odd lager, it probably wouldn't be a good idea, in his position as Chairman of Trustees, to be seen to encourage underage drinking among the staff. Biscuits then? A few of those big Christmas tins of shortbread and stuff, the kind with scenes from the Highlands on the lid that his mother used to buy. Maybe not. It was a bit like the lord of the manor distributing alms to the peasants. His mother had told him once that grand ladies often gave their maid servants Christmas gifts of cloth with which to make their uniforms. That must, he reflected, have been quite the most shite

Christmas gift of all time. A tin of shortbread would have been luxurious by comparison.

Inside, the department store was warm and bright. The Christmas songs, enjoining the shoppers to rock around the Christmas tree and to have themselves a merry little Christmas, played softly in the background. He made his way towards the special gifts section while he mulled over his conversation with Dick earlier. Dick clearly hadn't been pleased at Jeremy's suggestion that he call in at Fireside House to distribute some little gifts to the staff. He couldn't refuse but he obviously hadn't liked it. This new way of doing things, with the trustees becoming more involved with the Foundation, clearly didn't suit him at all. He wondered why not. Surely Dick's ego wasn't so fragile as all that. Although, he reflected, perhaps it was. From what Adam had told him, on a day to day basis Dick was lord of all he surveyed and none of the trustees ever visited Fireside House except by invitation for meetings. On appointment Adam had immediately broken that mould by turning up and introducing himself to the staff. As he had said to Jeremy, the women in the office were the people who really kept the Foundation going on a day to day basis. They managed all the case files, they processed applications and liaised with other charities as well as arranging property maintenance. They were the backbone of the charity and surely deserved some acknowledgement. Without them the everyday business would grind to a halt. Adam had also said that his personal impression was that if Dick went under a bus it would be months before anyone noticed in terms of his net contribution which, even on short acquaintance, Adam had gauged at roughly nil.

He moved towards the glittery display of toiletry gift sets and cast his eye over them. He picked up a pack of chocolate body paint and felt a bubble of laughter escape his lips. It would be wrong on so many levels that it was almost worth it, just so that he could see Dick implode. Reluctantly, he put the package back down again. Entertaining though the idea of an imploding Chief Executive might be, he needed to take his position seriously and whatever he thought of Dick, he needed to keep him on side for the moment. Also, Molly would kill him if she found out. He reached towards another stack of small gift boxes and then hesitated. Was he being a fool to get involved in all this? Molly would probably think so. He knew what she would say. Why not just let the police do their stuff? If there was anything to discover, they would discover it. It was their job and, after all, he didn't even officially take over as the Chairman of Trustees until the new year.

At the thought of his new role, the image of Adam rose before him. He could see him now, talking in the golf club bar, one hand wrapped round a pint of beer from which he took small steady sips. A tall slim man, neatly dressed in chinos and blue cashmere sweater, his serious grey eyes reflected his integrity and intelligence. Adam was no fool. He hadn't taken his role at the Foundation lightly and he certainly wasn't in it for the expenses or the prestige, like some of the trustees undoubtedly were. Jeremy experienced a sudden rush of regret, quickly followed by anger. He hadn't known Adam for very long but he had liked him. He had been good company. With similar backgrounds and interests in life, they could have been friends. Adam was a decent man and yet with all the fuss about Annie's murder, his death seemed to have slipped off the agenda for the time being. The poor man hadn't even had his funeral yet.

For the hundredth time, he ran his mind back to the day of the Foundation Christmas lunch, mentally ticking off the order of events, searching for something that he might have missed. On Adam's invitation, they had met the four managers in the bar beforehand. Adam had expressed his wish to get to know them better and a friendly pre-Christmas drink had seemed like the ideal opportunity. Okay, so far so good. So what had they talked about? The Foundation, obviously. The work that it did. Plans for the future. The stuff about the Lego buildings. But, he suddenly remembered, there had been a point at which a slight tension had arisen, he was sure of it. For a moment he stood perfectly still. He could hear Adam's voice now. He had been asking about how the properties were purchased and whether they had to meet certain criteria. And then he had said that he had noticed that most of the properties were purchased through one particular company. And in the split second that followed there had been what could only be described as an uncomfortable silence.

Picking up a dozen small boxes of Swiss chocolates, Jeremy made his way towards the tills, his expression thoughtful.

35

JEREMY CLIMBED the steps to Fireside House and looked in appreciation at the big wreath of holly and berries pinned to the door. From the bottom hung green and red glossy ribbons, fluttering slightly in the breeze. Whatever else he thought of Dick, he knew how to keep up appearances. It would only take a slight shift of the imagination to see Mr Pickwick emerging, figgy pudding in one hand and a foaming tankard in the other. Whatever was happening in the real world, as far as Dick was concerned it was business as usual at Fireside House and woe betide anybody who suggested otherwise.

He passed the bag containing the chocolates to his other hand, glad that he had remembered his gloves this morning. He had told Molly that he was just popping out to deliver some small Christmas gifts to the staff at Fireside House and she had looked up from her Weetabix with some suspicion. The previous evening she had started looking at short breaks online, commenting on how lovely they looked and how cheap they were, which was a sure sign that she thought he was overworking. What with that and the vitamins, which she counted out and placed ostentatiously by his tea mug every morning, he knew from experience that it was only a matter of time before she put her foot down. And Molly putting her foot down was a thing that she did rarely but was definitely not something to be taken lightly. She had been about to speak but had been distracted by Carlos asking her how people paid for things in the old days, before they had cards and phones and everything. Avoiding Carlos's eye, whom he suspected, in a show of solidarity, had deliberately created a diversion, he had slipped out before she could say anything.

He stepped back from the front door as it swung open and the receptionist beckoned him in.

"Mr Goodman, how lovely to see you."

Jeremy looked at her smiling face, his expression bordering on the dubious. She sounded as though she actually meant it. And perhaps, he thought, suddenly guilty, she did. He needed to reign himself in a bit. He was the newly appointed Chairman of Trustees, not Deputy Dawg.

The admin office was bright and cheerful, shiny decorations looped across the ceiling and tinsel draped across computers. In one corner a little artificial Christmas tree stood twinkling with pre-set fairy lights. Underneath a small pile of presents sat waiting to be opened. The chattering staff fell silent as he entered and all turned to look at him, their fingers halted over their keyboards. Yvette, the most senior of the women, rose from her chair to greet him.

"Mr Goodman. The Chief Executive said that you might drop in. Can we get you a coffee?"

"That's very kind of you," said Jeremy. He felt suddenly nervous at being the object of so much scrutiny. The last time he'd felt like this was as a student on his first teaching practice. He rustled into the bag which he had dropped on the floor. "Er, I bought you these. To say thank you and so on."

Fingers fumbling slightly, he pulled out the boxes of

chocolates and laid them on the desk nearest to him. He turned suddenly as the door was flung open and Dick blustered in.

"Ah, Goodman. Thought that was you at the door. Well girls," he looked round at the assembled women, of whom three at best could be described as girls with any accuracy. "I'm sure we've all got a lot to do before the holiday. Must clear the desks and so on and have everything shipshape for the new year. And we mustn't take up any more of the Chairman's time."

Jeremy looked at him with irritation. Dick was trying to hustle him out of the building and right now he didn't feel in the mood to be hustled.

"No hurry, Dick." He smiled pleasantly. "Two of the girls have just gone to make me a coffee."

He bit his lower lip. Unconsciously he had followed Dick's line and used the term 'girls', although as one of them was Lettie that had been despatched towards the kitchen perhaps he could be forgiven.

Dick's eyes narrowed and he glared at Yvette. The genial façade was starting to slip.

"It doesn't take two people to make a coffee."

Looking across at Yvette, Jeremy suddenly realised that in a building where a murder had occurred, it did indeed take two people to make a coffee. It was a fair bet that none of the women went anywhere alone, a notion which had completely failed to register with Dick. Yvette smiled sweetly back at Dick and remained silent.

"One or two matters that might need your attention for the new year," Dick said turning to Jeremy. He looked again at Yvette. "Ask the girl to bring the Chairman's coffee up to my office. Presumably it doesn't need two of you to do that."

And without waiting for a response he turned and gestured Jeremy towards the door. Irritated, Jeremy walked towards it. Short of a complete showdown, he really had no choice. Any idea that he might have had about talking to some of the staff about Foundation business, and in particular how property was purchased, was clearly busted. Following Dick back through the reception area, he glanced towards the basement door and shuddered. Dick might have had the decency to at least ensure that the door was closed. But no, it stood as it always did, propped open with the fire extinguisher.

In Dick's office Jeremy sat sipping at his coffee while he listened to Dick droning on about proposed publicity campaigns planned for the new year. Did the man actually have any idea what he was talking about? He seemed to be pretty much reading from a sheet in front of him. But he could have been reading from the bus timetable for all that it mattered. He had not wanted Jeremy in the main office and he had succeeded in getting him out of there. Round One to Dick, then. He glanced out of the window, his mind wandering as he drank his coffee and half-listened to the plans for the Foundation's exciting new year publicity campaign which seemed to include some celebrity that Jeremy had never heard of.

Suddenly he sat up straighter. Was that Aubrey out in the grounds? What on earth was he doing out there? And surely, that was Vincent with him? He watched as they slid from view and then replaced his cup and saucer carefully on the coaster which Dick had ostentatiously placed in front of him, as if he was the kind of barbarian that put hot cups down on polished surfaces. Standing up, he held out his hand.

"Well, Dick. That all sounds extremely promising. No doubt you'll bring all the trustees up to date at the next meeting."

36

───────

GLANCING up at Dick's office window, Jeremy could see him watching suspiciously, eyes narrowed, as he walked along the snowy gravel path. He resisted the urge to turn and wave at him. He had managed to keep up the façade of politeness and he wasn't about to drop it now. Dick might be stupid but even he would recognise a provocative action when he saw one. On reaching the ground floor, Jeremy had told the receptionist that he had a slight headache and would take a turn in the grounds before he left, and it was half true. He did have the beginnings of a headache, probably brought about by being out manoeuvred by a half-wit like Dick. That was the problem with stupid people, he thought. In spite of appearances to the contrary, they were actually much more difficult to deal with. It was something to do with their complete lack of sensitivity. He smiled ruefully as he thought of Dick's actually rather admirable strategy of getting him out of the main office. It was instinctive and cunning and relied on Jeremy not making a fuss. Which of course, he hadn't. He sighed. So much for getting any information out of the staff. He had barely been in there for more than three minutes before Dick had swept him out as effectively as a mine-sweeper.

He turned the corner and walked deeper into the shrubbery, partly to explore the grounds but mostly to escape Dick's prying eyes. It was, he thought, actually rather romantic out here. The shrubs were thick and luxuriant, even under their jackets of snow, and seemed to have been planted to give maximum privacy. Perhaps they had been, he thought. He let his imagination run free for a moment, an escape from his worries of moments earlier. This could have been where lovers had met in Sir George Renton's day, a servant girl tiptoeing out from the house to meet a boy from the town. A breathless kiss before she raced back to the kitchen, one hand holding up her white apron to keep it clean as she ran. Or perhaps one of Sir George Renton's daughters, perfumed and powdered, sneaking out to meet a stable lad, fearful of discovery by an outraged parent. Ah well, if all else failed, he could always try his hand at writing a romantic novel. He smiled and turned another corner, and then stopped.

Just ahead of him Lettie appeared to be leaning over something, a plastic carrier bag in her hand. He coughed loudly. He didn't want to walk up behind her and startle her. The girl had recently suffered enough shock to last her a lifetime. She turned as she heard him approaching.

"Oh, Mr Goodman."

She smiled. A fresh smile that showed her small white teeth and Jeremy thought again of the servant girl of his imagination going out to the shrubbery to meet her lover. He smiled back. He found himself suddenly wondering what she would do with her life. Whether she would stay at the Foundation, as many of the other women had. Or perhaps she would do something else, something different. He wondered how many GCSE's she had gained at school and if she had considered going to college, or evening classes perhaps, with a view to gaining further qualifications. Perhaps he ought to talk to her about it. He gave himself a mental shake. Once a teacher, always a teacher. Although, to be fair, the words staff and development were unlikely to have ever cropped up in any sentence uttered by Dick.

"What are you doing out here, Lettie?"

"Oh, nothing wrong, Mr Goodman. Honestly. I asked Yvette if I could and she said that it was all right. She's watching from the window," she added.

Her cheeks flushed as she spoke and she moved aside slightly to reveal a small stone statue of a cherub, its outstretched arms holding a bird bath above its head, its chubby little body covered in grey green lichen. Jeremy glanced across and saw Yvette framed in the downstairs office window.

"I was putting some feed out for the birds." The girl spoke in a rush, anxious to explain herself before she was accused "Annie always did it and I remembered it this morning and thought that probably nobody else had thought of it. I was worried that the birds would be missing it. What with the snow and everything."

She trailed off and stared at him.

"That's very thoughtful of you, Lettie. I'm sure that the birds will appreciate it. Do you get many birds in the grounds?"

Lettie relaxed slightly and dropped the bag of bird food at her feet.

"Mostly robins at this time of year. And magpies," she added. She looked around as she spoke as if searching for proof to verify her story.

As if in answer, a magpie flew to a branch above Jeremy's head and began to clack loudly. Together they watched the bird in silence for a few moments.

"One for sorrow," said Lettie. "That's what my mum says.

And two for joy," she added brightly as another magpie joined its mate on the branch.

We could all do with some of that, thought Jeremy. But out here, away from listening ears, it might just be the perfect time and place to get some information.

"Lettie," he spoke slowly, feeling his way. "What is that you actually do at the Foundation? I mean, do you deal with the people that the Foundation house? Or other charities perhaps?

"Oh, no." Lettie sounded shocked. "I just input stuff on the files and things like that. And sometimes make phone calls, to get information and so on when Yvette asks me to."

"Right." Jeremy nodded encouragingly. "And do you see all the files?"

"I think so, yes."

"So would you know, for instance, when a property has been purchased?"

Lettie nodded enthusiastically.

"Yes, because I have to open up a new file and input all the details."

Jeremy looked at her thoughtfully. He didn't want to push her too far. She seemed like a bright kind of girl and might very easily start wondering why he was asking her all these questions. On the other hand, he might not have a chance like this again.

"What sort of details?"

"Oh, the address. And how many bedrooms it has and so on. Whether it requires any alteration or renovation and then who we've invited to quote for the work. And then I have to keep it updated, like when any work on it is finished and it's ready to be let, who the tenants are, what the rent is and so on."

"And do you make a note of who the Foundation purchased it from?"

"Yes. That's the next thing after the address."

"I see." He tried to keep his tone casual but he could feel his excitement mounting. "And is it always the same people?"

"There's one company that the managers often buy property from."

"Ah. And what's the name of that company?"

He held his breath.

"Henry Holdings."

37

———————

AUBREY, Vincent and Eric watched from the shadow of the ice house as Jeremy and Lettie walked towards them. Lettie's clear high voice drifted across the cold air

"It's called an ice house. I found it when I was out here exploring one day during my lunch hour."

Jeremy glanced sideways at her. Lots of girls of her age would spend their lunch hour reading magazines or shopping. Compared to most of them, she really was hardly more than a child. It probably wasn't that long ago that she was still playing with dolls.

"I asked Yvette what it was," Lettie continued. "They used to keep ice in it," she added.

Jeremy nodded as they approached the low squat building. The cats moved further back into the bushes.

"What's it used for now?"

"I don't know. I don't think that it's used for anything." She glanced back towards the house, her expression slightly worried. "I think I'd better get back. Yvette will be wondering what I'm doing."

"Yes, perhaps you better had."

It wasn't Yvette that he was concerned about though. If Dick discovered that she'd been out here talking to him she'd probably get into trouble. Not only for talking to him but for being outside at all during working hours. As far as Dick was concerned, the place of the office staff was in the office unless and until told otherwise.

He watched as she ran towards the house, her small figure flying across the snow. Her face, when she had uttered the words Henry Holdings had been completely innocent. It obviously didn't ring any alarm bells with her. Or indeed any of the other staff who presumably also had access to the files. So why had the mention of purchasing properties made the senior managers so uncomfortable? Were they somehow involved in this Henry Holdings company? But why would they be? They were all successful. They were all paid well. They had all, as far as he could tell, landed a pretty cushy number at the Foundation.

He swept the snow from a small bench and sat down, feeling the damp chill of the stone as it rose up through the fabric of his coat. The cogs in his brain began to gently spin and whir as he stared down at the small paw prints in the snow. His own experience of life had taught him that the most unlikely people were corruptible. The amounts didn't even have to be that big. In fact, the temptation to steal was not so much on the amount gained as on what could be done with it. For somebody who couldn't pay a fifty pound parking fine, the temptation to put the hand in the till might be considerable.

The face of Beth, the erstwhile school secretary of Sir Frank Wainwright Comprehensive, floated before him. A mild-mannered, gentle woman of indeterminate years, she wore glasses and had the kind of hair that looked as if it was carefully curled once a week at her local hairdresser. She was popular with both staff and pupils. Always kindly, always ready to lend a listening ear, even when some of the most outrageous school scoundrels claimed to have lost their bus fare home and needed a quid from school funds, which they then promptly spent with the school fag barons. And yet she had quietly and systematically siphoned off several thousand pounds from the school accounts. As a consequence, she had been sentenced to four months. As the magistrate had said, it was the breach of trust as much as the theft that had influenced his decision to impose a custodial sentence. She hadn't even been particularly sorry as far as Jeremy could tell. She had certainly failed to express any remorse even if she hadn't felt it, a gesture which might have made the magistrate a little more sympathetic towards her.

At the time they had all been completely astonished. Beth, of all people. Nice sweet-natured Beth who could always be relied upon to hand out a cup of tea and a few paracetamol to staff with a hangover. Even the kids, most of whom weren't averse to cutting out the middle man when it came to paying for goods, had been appalled. The Head, with her usual talent for ineptitude and getting things wrong, had forbidden all discussion of the subject. Mostly, Jeremy suspected, in an effort to deflect any criticism of her own role in the debacle. In any event, it was an edict which the pupils, and most of the staff, had simply ignored. From the heated debates that had taken place in his own classroom Jeremy had gathered that stealing from your own was not done. It had actually been quite gratifying to discover that the pupils considered Sir Frank's as 'one of their own' and for a short time there was something that might even have been considered a truce between staff and pupils. It hadn't lasted long. In fact, only until the Head had banned the annual coach trip to the seaside in revenge for Year Ten pupils being caught breaking into a cupboard and stealing chemicals from one of the labs. Wisely, nobody had asked them what they wanted the chemicals for.

The most galling thing was that what Beth had done hadn't

even been all that clever. All it had taken was a lack of managerial eyes on the ball and the willingness to take a risk. It had been acknowledged later by the Head, albeit reluctantly and in the face of incontrovertible evidence, that the school's financial affairs were wide open to abuse. Beth was responsible for ordering stationery and other sundry items. Staff simply passed their requests to her which she then processed. Nobody checked on anything, himself included. As long as the right amount of exercise books or art materials arrived, as long as any equipment was properly serviced or updated when required, that was all that they were interested in.

Without fail, the right amount of materials did arrive, along with appropriate servicing and updating of all equipment. From Beth's brother, who owned a school's supply and servicing business. It was so simple that it was almost laughable. The brother simply whacked fifty percent on top of the real cost and the pair split it between them. Beth hadn't been stupid though. The items had been genuinely ordered. There was a proper paper trail. Everything was neatly filed. It was just, given what Sir Frank's was paying for them, they should have come gold-plated. And what had she wanted the money for? A conservatory apparently and a holiday 'somewhere nice'.

And she would have got her wish if a new governor hadn't started looking at the school accounts and queried why Sir Frank's seemed to be paying so much for standard items. He had asked why they didn't cast around a bit more to see if they could get a better discount. Following which, a little digging into the brother's company had revealed that Beth was a director, after which the wheels had started to fall fairly rapidly off the bus. It was a simple method, but it worked. Had it also worked for Henry Holdings? Jeremy thought that it had. Using the same formula, albeit on a bigger scale, it seemed likely that this Henry Holdings company was buying property and then selling it to the Foundation at a considerable mark-up and that the managers were somehow involved. They had certainly looked uncomfortable when Adam had mentioned it. So what, he wondered, was the lure for them?

He thought about what he knew about them. Like the office staff, it was actually very little. What he did know, because Adam had told him, was that they were all earning enough to pay for most of life's little luxuries without feeling the pinch. Perhaps it was just greed. Perhaps whatever they had, they wanted more. Also, he knew, some people just couldn't resist an opportunity when it presented itself. Like when he had asked Tommy Wade, having been caught on camera stealing fifty pounds from a handbag that had been left at a bus station, why he had done it. He had been met with a look of pure astonishment and the simple yet eloquent reply, 'well, I had to Sir, didn't I? I mean, like, it was there'.

And perhaps the same answer was true of the senior managers. Had they been syphoning off funds from the Foundation simply 'because they were there'? Suddenly Dick's lack of managerial skills and obvious lack of grasp of the affairs of the Foundation, seemed rather more than just tiresome. If what he suspected was true, then it was downright negligent. But if he was right, if the managers were somehow involved in this Henry Holdings company, surely the fear of discovery wouldn't be sufficient to lead to murder? Despite his doubts, he was beginning to have a horrible feeling that it might be. As ever, it would depend on what the ultimate reward might be.

The headache that he had pleaded to the receptionist earlier began to take on more reality. He got up from the bench and turned towards the ice house. The entrance, only half-blocked by the broken iron gate, was easily accessible. He pushed aside the branches and stepped inside, followed seconds later by the three cats.

Aubrey turned to Vincent.

"What's he doing?"

Vincent shrugged.

"Exploring?"

They watched as Jeremy walked further into the ice house, his hands touching the walls as he felt his way forward.

38

———————

Harry reached across the table and poured himself another glass of red wine. Tomorrow. Definitely. Tomorrow he would cut down. Start counting the number of units he was drinking, start making a conscious effort. Although the last time he had looked at the NHS guidelines it had been something that, in his opinion, was frankly ludicrous. A maximum of fourteen units a week? That was only two glasses a day and sometimes he felt so stressed that the first two glasses didn't even touch the sides. But tomorrow. Tomorrow he would start to change his ways. Because, after all, tomorrow was another day and he had everything to look forward to.

He looked back down at the map spread out on his lap. He could do this online, he knew, but there was something very satisfying about a paper map. It had a permanence to it that gave his dream a reality. His finger hovered over the town of Northampton again. He had narrowed his choices down to three but the more he had thought about it, the more he was starting to feel that Northampton might be just what he was looking for. It seemed to be a fairly vibrant place; it had good transport links, some of its traditional industries seemed to have died off but other decent businesses had sprung up. It also had a university which presumably contained business students as well as some creatives. Lots of students wanted an industry placement, somewhere they could gain some practical experience. Well, he was in a prime position to give it to them. He'd learned a lot in his years in the business. They wouldn't be disappointed, they would get as much from him as he did from them. Also on the plus side, he didn't know anybody there, he wasn't even sure that he'd ever been there, but that was all to the good.

Everything would be new. He could start again with a fresh slate. Starting again with a fresh slate was meat and drink to him. He'd done it often enough in the past. On the coffee table next to him his mobile began ringing. He ignored it. It wouldn't be anybody that he wanted to speak to. Probably a text telling him that someone had just tried to access an account that he didn't have, with a bank that he'd never banked with, but all would be well if he just clicked on the link and provided them with a few personal details. Such as his date of birth and pin numbers. Did anybody still fall for that, he wondered? He guessed that they must do or the scams wouldn't keep coming. Like much else in life, he supposed. It was a numbers game. You didn't need lots of trusting innocents, just some.

Draining his glass he placed the map to one side and stood up. He looked around him at the state of the art sound system and the tastefully expensive furnishings. It reminded him of nothing so much as an upmarket hotel room. Would he be sorry to leave it? Not really. He'd bought it as an investment but had never really felt particularly warm towards it. In fact, if he was honest with himself, the only place that he had ever felt attached to was his old attic room when he'd lived with the women. It had been the first time he had been safe, warm and unafraid. What he had here was what had been described as an executive upmarket property, suitable for a family and situated in what was generally thought to be a good area of the town. He didn't think that he'd have much trouble selling it. He hadn't done anything to it but he hadn't needed to. Everything had been in good working order when he had moved in, in fact that was pretty much what had attracted him to it. All this DIY stuff had never held much of a pull for him. He couldn't see the point. Why do it yourself when you could pay someone else to do it?

He reached for the wine bottle and poured himself another glass. The day he had moved in here had been about as different to today as it was possible to be. Then it had been a bright summer day, flowers had been out in the garden and the previous owners had left him a bottle of wine and a welcome card. He had been oddly touched, it had been such an unexpected gesture. It hadn't occurred to him to do anything similar for the purchaser of his flat in London. In fact, he wasn't sure that he had even met the person who had bought it. Everything, including viewings, had been done through the agents. Buying it after his last divorce, in reality it hadn't been much more than a crash pad. Somewhere to sleep between working and socialising. These days he left the office at five along with everybody else, unless he was on security duty in which case he left at ten past five, and came home to watch films and drink wine.

He'd tried some of the pubs in town but mostly they'd been full of youngsters, vying with each other to see who could drink the most shots without falling over. The alternative was the kind of boozer that the old codgers hung about in and he didn't think that he'd got to that stage yet. But Northampton would be different. It wasn't a city but it was a big town. It would have restaurants and bars, theatres, the kind of vibrancy that this town lacked. He hesitated for a moment. Maybe he was kidding himself. He wasn't a young man about town anymore. But, he thought, suddenly brightening again, he wasn't dead yet. There was time still for some fun.

He walked towards the window and pulled the curtains across, shutting out the cold wintery light of the snowy night. Picking up the remote, he flicked on the electric wood burner and watched the artificial flames flicker up. He found himself increasingly wondering these days where all the time had gone. He had worked in his last post for over ten years and it already seemed like a life time ago. He had enjoyed his time there, though. Within a fairly short space of time he'd got his feet well and truly under the table and had secured some lucrative accounts with an impressive client list. He had definitely been the golden boy. But, gradually, bit by bit, he had started to notice tiny changes. There had been a few after work drinking sessions that he hadn't been invited to, some meetings which had been held while he was on annual leave and about which nobody had thought to update him, a client conference at which he hadn't been invited to speak. Toughest of all, a few campaigns had been passed to others which he had considered by rights should have been headed by him. The younger staff no longer seemed to try to please him as they once had. At one time barely a day had gone by without one or other of them finding an excuse to drop by his office. In his last year there they seemed to have forgotten where his office was. But he could see the writing on the wall when it presented itself. The young Turks were pushing themselves forward. He was an old campaigner, literally. He could smell ambition a mile off. He'd been one of them himself once.

Even so, he hadn't felt too threatened. He was a wily old fox and the agency still valued his experience, to say nothing of his contacts. But then had come the last recession and there had been rumours of redundancies. Suddenly his position no longer seemed quite so secure and for the first time he scented danger. His interest in the vacancies section of PR Week grew.

Mentally sifting through the possibilities on the ground that it was better to jump than be pushed, at first he had barely glanced at the Foundation's advertised vacancy for the new post of Public Relations and Marketing Manager. It was in some place on the south coast, a town that he had no desire to visit let alone live in, and it seemed to be some kind of charity. What did he know about charities? He moved strictly in the world of corporate and commercial. Glancing over the advert and already starting to skim the next one, he had almost missed the salary. And then he had done a double-take. It was almost a third more than he was earning now, plus a car, plus health care. Suddenly the idea of living in a small town on the south coast didn't seem quite so bad after all.

39

———————

MAX THREW his phone across the kitchen table. Where the hell was Harry? And why wasn't he answering his phone? They had taken to not speaking to each unnecessarily at work, just in case they were overheard, but he needed to talk to him now. He wanted to know what Harry thought that Jeremy was doing at Fireside House today. Dick had said that he was delivering some Christmas presents for the staff but Max doubted it. Nobody had done such a thing before, why would they start now? Was this Jeremy going to start sticking his nose in like Adam had done? He picked up his phone again and scrolled through the list of contacts. Perhaps he'd have better luck with Nigel. He tapped impatiently on the table top as he waited for Nigel to answer.

"Max."

"Nigel."

For a moment there was silence and then Max spoke again. No point pretending this was a social call.

"Why do you think that the Chairman of Trustees was at the Foundation today?"

"Poking about, I should think."

Max resisted the urge to start shouting. Of course he had been poking about. Why did Nigel always have to state the bloody obvious? He swallowed and struggled to keep his voice very calm.

"Do you think that he found anything?"

"Such as?"

"I don't bloody know. Anything."

"I doubt it. And Max, it's probably best if we don't ring each other."

Throwing the phone down on the table, Max made his way out to the garden. In the shed, surrounded by his paintings and drawings, he felt himself relax slightly. He dropped his shoulders and breathed in deeply, inhaling the familiar smell of his oils and canvases, relishing the mingling of scents with the ghost of old compost bags and clods of earth clinging to garden forks left there by his father. Since his death his stepmother had taken over the gardening and he had been happy to leave her to it. He had even put up a new shed to keep her out of the old one. But over the last year she had spent more time watching detective show re-runs on the television and done less and less in the garden. He had a sinking feeling that before too long he would have to get a gardener, particularly if he wanted to sell the place.

Selling the place. That was the plan. But how was he going to get her out? The last time he had tried to raise the idea of each of them buying something smaller she had reacted angrily and accused him of trying to push her out of her home. Which, of course, he was. But not out into the cold street, not to some back water, much as the idea appealed. With what they realised on the house, she could easily afford to buy herself a smart little apartment near the centre of town, somewhere easy to manage and closer to what little action there was. She had been droning on recently about never going out or seeing anyone, as if her isolation was his fault. He had resisted the urge to point out that she would need to get washed and dressed first, to stop looking like the poster girl for bag ladies. But of course, she didn't really want to go out or see anybody. What she really wanted was to make life difficult for him. Which she did, at every available opportunity. And, he reluctantly admitted to himself, he had started to repay her in kind. Last night, when he was returning from the pub, he had deliberately revved his engine on the drive and slammed the garage door shut as hard as he could. He had been rewarded by the sight of the light snapping on in her bedroom and her angry face appearing at the window. It had been a petty act of retaliation, and one which he didn't like himself for, but he had to admit that it had been satisfying.

Reaching under the trestle table that stood across one wall and on which Eric sat regarding him with solemn amber eyes, he pulled out a bottle of whisky and a small glass. He sat silently and brooded as he sipped at his drink, feeling his chest start to relax as the whisky burned down his throat. Why did everything have to start falling apart just when it had all been going so well? As long as Dick and the trustees had minded their own business, they had been perfectly safe. If only Charles hadn't decided to retire. If only Adam hadn't been appointed as Chairman of the Trustees. And now there was this bloody Jeremy bloke to worry about. How much did he know? He shook himself. What was done was done. He just had to hold his nerve. Anyway, things weren't so bad. When they had formed Henry Holdings they had agreed on a five year plan after which they would wind it down. They would have to finish a year earlier than they had planned but that was all right. They'd done well. Very well. He'd amassed more money than he would ever have thought possible and what with that and the sale of the house, the island life of his dreams would be easily within his reach.

He took another sip of his whisky and looked across at Eric who had now fallen asleep. How easy was it, he wondered, to get a pet passport.

40

____

Aubrey settled himself more comfortably across Jeremy's lap and nudged his hand with his head. Jeremy stretched his legs and rewarded him by running his hand down his thick fur. Opposite him Molly sat on the sofa, her legs tucked beneath her as she gazed into the fire. For several minutes the three of them sat in companionable silence.

"You didn't tell me what you bought for the staff at Fireside House," said Molly. "What did you decide on?"

"Some little boxes of Swiss chocolates."

Molly nodded in approval.

"Of course, Dick had to interfere," Jeremy continued. "I'd hardly got inside the door before he came bustling in. He couldn't wait to get me out of there."

"Why?" Molly sounded puzzled. "What's it to him if you choose to give the staff a little gift? Families often bring gifts into the Lodge for the carers and I'm always pleased for them. Pleased that they're appreciated."

"Well, it's Dick's little kingdom isn't it? Lord of all he surveys. If there's any largesse to distribute then he has to be the one distributing it. When the Christmas bonuses are paid,

Adam told me that Dick expects the staff to personally thank him. It's not even his money. Do you know, the more I get to know him, the more I'm beginning to rather dislike him. He reminds me of Clive."

Aubrey tucked his head under his paw. It was his default reaction whenever Jeremy's erstwhile colleague, the loathsome Clive and his equally repellent wife Rachel were mentioned.

"Only Dick is less intelligent," Jeremy continued. He hesitated. He had decided earlier not to tell Molly what he had discovered this morning on the basis that she would worry, and so far he had stuck to the decision. All through dinner they had talked about Molly's work at Lilac Tree Lodge and his scheduled inspections for the new year. But the concept of keeping things from her was so alien that he now felt the words burbling out before he could stop them. "Anyway, when I left Fireside House I did some exploring in the grounds."

Molly's mouth tightened and she reached down and scooped up Vincent who had suddenly appeared from behind the closed curtains. Aubrey grinned. Vincent was brilliant at being unobserved. He could never really manage it himself. He always gave himself away one way or another. Usually when he thought that there might be a food opportunity on the horizon. He listened as Jeremy continued talking. He knew what Jeremy was going to tell Molly. He and Vincent had followed him through the ice house, keeping to the shadows, and watching as he came across the opening to the tunnel.

Jeremy held up his hands in mock surrender and grinned.

"I know, I know. Anyway, I ran into that girl Lettie, the one who found Annie's body. She was feeding the birds. And she told me about an ice house in the shrubbery so I decided to take a look."

"How did you get in?"

"It was easy, it was open. So I went inside and it was just a sort of dome-shaped brick building. Big enough for me to stand up in but not loads of room. So I walked further in and there it was."

"There was what?"

"An opening to a tunnel."

"Did you go in?" Molly sounded interested now.

Jeremy nodded.

"I did. And you'll never guess where it lead to."

Molly shook her head.

"No. Where?"

"Into the basement. Inside the house."

Molly stared at him.

"But that means…"

"I know. That's the thing that's been on my mind. I kept thinking, given where the door to the basement is, whoever went down there after Annie was taking a mammoth risk. There's ten or so women in the main office and the door to their cloakroom is opposite the door to the basement. But if the murderer knew about the tunnel then there was no risk at all."

"But wouldn't somebody have spotted him going out or coming in to the house? The receptionist or somebody?"

"No. Because you can go out through the back. It leads straight into the grounds."

"So who knew about the tunnel?"

"That, my dearest Molly, is the million dollar question. Of course," he added. "It's possible that they all knew about it."

Molly nodded.

"I suppose so. Was it creepy down there?"

"Very." Jeremy gave a slight theatrical shudder and grinned. "To be honest Moll, I was a bit scared. I thought about turning back but I really wanted to know what was at the end of it."

Molly smiled. Jeremy's boyish enthusiasm for an adventure had never quite left him. It was one of the things that was so loveable about him. Even if he did make her worry sometimes. He had told her once about him sneaking out at night one Halloween when he was aged nine. His parents had been watching television downstairs and he had gone with two friends to cook sausages over a camp fire and tell ghost stories in the small wood near his home. Finding a small clearing they had searched around for some twigs to start the fire and had managed to disturb a startled tramp who had jumped up and shouted at them. In running away Jeremy had tripped and fallen over some broken glass which had resulted in a dozen stitches to his leg. He still had the scar. But, typical Jeremy, he had gone back the next night to say sorry to the tramp for startling him and given him a bar of chocolate.

"And then when I came out into the basement," Jeremy continued, "I felt even more scared. Because, well, you know. Being in a place where you know that somebody has died, and died horribly, is really frightening. Why people go on those Jack the Ripper tour things in Whitechapel is beyond me. Why would you want to stare at a spot where some poor woman has been horribly butchered? Anyway, at first, I didn't even know that it was the basement. It was just a big gloomy space. I walked about a bit and then I saw the shelving with the files stacked on them and realised where I was."

"Was it cold?"

"Yes, sort of chilly, if you know what I mean."

Molly nodded.

"I don't suppose that there's any point in heating it." She tickled the back of Vincent's head. "Have the police finished with it now?"

"I guess so. I didn't see any police tape or anything. When I realised where I was, I didn't hang around for too long. I just went back along the tunnel and out through the ice house into the grounds. I thought it might give the receptionist a bit of a shock if I suddenly appeared from nowhere. It was a real relief to get out into the fresh air again. No wonder the staff don't like going down there."

They like it even less now, thought Aubrey. According to Eric, the staff were a lot more shaken by Annie's murder than had been allowed for. Given that it was dark by about four o'clock, the women now left the office as a group and didn't separate until they were within the safety of the high street and street lamps. Even within the building, none of them ventured anywhere alone. Visiting the cloakroom or the kitchen, they travelled in pairs. And as for the basement, it was completely out of bounds. For a cat however, it was the perfect place. Dark, cool, lots of shadows and places to hide plus a hidden exit. But for people, it was probably the stuff of nightmares.

What people liked, Aubrey knew, was space and light, and, without being blessed with the eyes of a cat, the ability to see all around them. Especially when a brutal murder had taken place. He thought suddenly of Annie, of her lying down there cold and dead. He would miss her. They all would. And not just because she had fed them. She had talked to them often when they were down in the kitchen with her, making themselves comfortable and curling around each other in the cardboard box into which she had placed an old cushion.

"Of course, I always took him back," she would say, as she busied herself with sorting the tea mugs. "He was always sorry and I always took him back. More fool me," she would add but without a trace of bitterness. "I suppose in some ways he couldn't help it. Some men can't. And of course, he was very handsome. He always dressed nice, if you know what I mean." And a wistful expression would drift across her weathered face as she thought about the man who always dressed nice. "When he was took, it was funny, I kept expecting him to walk back through the door. But of course, he never did. But you get used to being on your own, don't you?"

And Aubrey had to agree. You did get used to being on your own. It was just a different way of being.

41

———————

MOLLY USHERED the woman before her and directed her to the chair next to the fire as Jeremy switched off the television and rose to greet her.

"Here, let me take your coat."

The woman slowly unbuttoned her coat and sat down. She folded her hands together and stared for a moment at the Christmas tree. A look of pain crossed her face. She turned to Molly.

"I hope that you don't mind me coming round like this. Only I thought that Jeremy might like these." Reaching down, she pulled a cardboard wallet folder from the large leather bag that she had been carrying. "I found them when I was searching for some insurance documents in Adam's desk."

Jeremy reached forward to take the folder, noting as he did so the papery whiteness of the woman's face. He flicked open the folder and ran his hands across the papers.

"What are they?"

"Documents and so on from the Foundation. I'm not sure exactly what's in there but Dick told me that you'll be taking over as the new Chairman of Trustees."

"That's very thoughtful of you," said Molly. "Only you needn't have driven all the way over here. Jeremy could have picked them up."

"Oh, no. That's fine. I wanted to. It's good to get out for a while."

"Of course," said Jeremy. "Let me fetch you a drink. Wine? Or coffee perhaps if you're driving?"

Molly settled herself on the sofa and regarded their visitor as Jeremy busied himself in the kitchen. A tall woman with thick dark shoulder length hair, lightly frosted with grey, and fine regular features, albeit ravaged with grief. She was dressed in a classically simple skirt and sweater, the kind that cost a fortune and always look good. Her name, Audrey, suited her too, thought Molly. Slightly old-fashioned for a woman of her age, nevertheless, it fitted her. There was something both grave and elegant about it. Audrey and Adam. They must have been quite the couple. She found herself wondering if Audrey worked and, if so, what she did. Something serious. Something dignified, without a doubt. A researcher or a consultant or something. Her two sons, she knew, were at university, one studying law, the other accountancy, although they must be home for the Christmas holiday by now.

"How are you coping? Are you managing all right?"

Molly's tone was gentle, her expression one of kindly concern. There was no ignoring the fact of Adam's death, it hovered in the room like a hesitant visitor. The usual enquiries as to how ready Audrey was for Christmas or whether she was doing anything nice would go down like the proverbial lead one.

Molly's tone was gentle. Audrey swallowed before replying and when she spoke her voice was low.

"Yes, pretty much thank you, although it all still seems unreal. Sometimes, I wake in the morning and for a few seconds I feel happy. And then I remember." She paused and clasped her hands together. "It's odd how some people have reacted though. The other day I saw an old friend in the high street and I'm almost sure that she crossed the road to avoid me."

"She probably just didn't see you," said Molly, although, she thought, she probably did. Some people, not knowing what to say to a recently bereaved person, didn't say anything at all.

"It doesn't help that it's nearly Christmas," Audrey continued. "Adam loved Christmas." She smiled slightly, a faint flickering of the mouth. "He always wanted to get the decorations out way too early. If I'd let him he would have had the tree up in November."

Molly felt a sudden pang. Things were bad enough for Audrey. But to have to go through such a terrible experience at this time of the year, when everyone was in festive mood and wishing each other a merry Christmas, must be sheer hell. She had never really suffered bereavement herself, not seriously anyway. Both her parents were still alive and her older brother, although living in Australia with his family, was thriving. Three of her grandparents had died when she was really too young to remember them and the fourth had passed away peacefully in his bed aged ninety-five. She couldn't really begin to imagine what Audrey might be going through. It was bad enough that her husband had died, but to have died in such circumstances was truly dreadful. She searched for something else to say.

"It must be a comfort to have your sons with you."

"Yes." Audrey smiled again, a fuller smile this time that softened her features and showed the attractive woman that she really was. "They've been wonderful. They'll be staying until after the funeral."

"You have a date then?"

Audrey nodded.

"The tenth of January." She grimaced slightly. "It seems

like such a long way off. I don't know if I'm glad or sorry. Part of me wants, needs, to get it over with. Yet another part feels that as long as it doesn't happen, then Adam hasn't really gone."

Molly remained silent. There didn't really seem to be anything to say to that. When Audrey spoke again, her voice was so low that Molly had to struggle to hear it.

"The police haven't actually said to me that it was murder, not in so many words." She stared at Molly, the anguish stamped across her face. "But everybody knows that it was. I just don't understand why. What did Adam ever do to anybody?"

———

MOLLY LAY ASIDE the book that she was reading as Jeremy came into the bedroom. His face looked strained as he sat on the edge of the bed.

"I've been looking through those documents that Adam's wife brought round."

"And?"

"Moll, there's definitely dark goings on at the Foundation. I mean aside from the body count."

Molly sat up straighter and stared at him.

"What sort of dark goings on? What was in the folder?"

"Well, there was some archive material. Adam was probably trying to get a feel for the work of the Foundation. You know, old newsletters that were sent out to supporters of the charity, updating them on the work that had been done, that kind of thing. There were minutes of meetings as well. Nothing, on the face of it, very interesting. It seemed to be mostly the managers giving updates on activities, properties purchased, publicity campaigns and so on, and the trustees just listening. Pretty routine stuff. Except for the last meeting, the one that I attended. At the time I didn't realise that there was anything particularly different about it. It was only when I read the minutes of previous meetings that it really struck me."

"And?"

"Well, I think I told you before that Adam was asking questions. If the previous meeting minutes are accurate, that was something that the Chairman just didn't do. None of the trustees did, really"

"What, never?"

"Well, only conventional ones such as how many tenants the Foundation now had or when was the next publicity campaign scheduled for. Nothing controversial. In fact, you could more or less interchange any of the minutes of previous meetings, they were so similar. They all more or less reported the same things, new legacies, properties purchased, planned publicity campaigns and so on. But on that last one, after listening to the managers reports, Adam was probing a bit further. There's another thing." Jeremy paused and drew breath. "He made some notes. They're in the back of the folder in a little notebook. Hold on, I'll fetch it."

Molly watched as he left the room and headed towards his study. She couldn't stop him now, even if she tried. Adventure aside, Jeremy would, she knew, consider it his duty to put right any wrongs that had been committed. And, she had to concede, it probably was. Up to a point. But if crimes had been committed then it was a matter for the police. She got up and put her dressing gown on. The early night she had promised herself would have to wait. Jeremy turned as she entered the study.

"I'll go and stoke up the fire."

42

————————

Downstairs, Molly sat on the sofa and huddled into her dressing gown while Jeremy stood leaning against the mantlepiece, the small black notebook in his hand. They both turned their heads at the sound of the key in the lock and Carlos came in rubbing his hands together.

"How was it?" asked Molly.

"It was okay. A bit boring really. Most of college was there. They had a band and that."

"And did you walk home with some of the others as we asked?"

Carlos nodded. He had reached the age where he wasn't keen on Molly or Jeremy picking him up but they always insisted that, whenever possible, he didn't walk alone after dark even when it was a relatively short distance. Lads walking through the town on their own at night were liable to attract trouble and while he could hold his own in a fair fight, Molly and Jeremy were well aware of the little gangs that sometimes sat drinking cider and strong lager on the beach and then wandered into town to cause trouble.

"Rubble and Jake live just along the way. I walked with them." He yawned. "I think I'll go up to bed."

They watched as he left the room and listened to the slow tread of his step on the stairs. Jeremy raised his eyebrows.

"He's missing Teddy," Molly said. "And the last couple of times that he's tried to WhatsApp her, she hasn't been there."

"Do you think she's met someone else?"

Molly shrugged.

"Who knows? But if she has, I wish that she'd tell him and put him out of his misery."

"Well, he won't be the first teenage boy to get his heart broken. He'll get over it."

Molly looked thoughtful.

"I'm not so sure." She fell silent for a moment. "Anyway, what's in this notebook?"

Jeremy flicked the book open.

"Well, it's just sort of brief notes but Adam specifically mentions Henry Holdings."

"Henry who?"

"Henry Holdings. It's a property company, one that the Foundation buys a lot of their properties from. Not all of them, but a good few."

Molly looked thoughtful.

"Right. So what does he say about it?"

Jeremy dipped his head and began reading.

"Right. Well, the first note just says 'do more checks on recent properties purchased' but then it becomes more expansive and says 'who or what is Henry Holdings? Why do the Foundation buy their property through them?' But then Moll, it gets really interesting."

Molly nodded.

"Go on."

"Do you remember a month or so ago you were just browsing the internet and you decided to check out our old house, and saw that it had been sold again? Well, it seems that for most properties you can find a sort of history of a house in terms of sale price over the years."

"And that's what Adam found for the Foundation properties?"

"Exactly. For example, one property was purchased for a hundred and twenty thousand but six months later the Foundation bought the same property from Henry Holdings for three hundred thousand. And the Foundation are always cash buyers. Even given inflation, property prices don't rise that quickly."

"But surely somebody would have noticed? One of the other trustees, or the previous chairman?"

Jeremy shook his head.

"Apparently not. All the purchasing and operational matters are left to the managers."

"So what do the trustees actually do?"

"Turn up and claim expenses from what I can gather. From reading the minutes of meetings they just seem to nod everything through."

"So who do you think is behind this Henry Holdings?"

Jeremy looked serious.

"Somebody at the Foundation." He hesitated. "I think it must be one of the four managers. It has to be."

"Or all of them," pointed out Molly. "It must be, or there was the risk that one of the other managers would have found out. So do you think that they realised that Adam was on to them? But what about Annie? What did she have to do with it?"

Jeremy closed the notebook and sat next to her on the sofa.

"I don't really know. I'm guessing that she either knew something or hinted that she did. She was a bit like that. You know, one of those 'oh wouldn't you like to know' types. But there was no harm in her really."

"But surely…" Molly hesitated. "I mean you wouldn't kill somebody…"

"It depends on the circumstances." Jeremy looked thoughtful. "Don't forget, it's not just the money. It's the lifestyle, the job, the whole lot. And then there's the prospect of prison. Judges take a very dim view of theft from employers. And don't forget that this particular employer is a charity. I mean, think about it. That would go down a storm with the average jury. If Henry Holdings was exposed there'd be no coming back from it. Although," he added, "they might not all have been responsible for the deaths of Adam and Annie. It could be just one of them. The one with the most to lose."

Molly nodded.

"I suppose so. But how did they do it? How did they manage this Henry Holdings business? Can anybody just set up a company?"

"Well, not just anybody. But it's much easier than you might think. And a limited company is an excellent screen to hide behind."

"So what now?"

"I'm going to see what I can find out about Henry Holdings. It's got a company number so it must have been registered. That means that there is at least some information out there although I doubt that whoever is behind this has used their own names."

"Jeremy, be careful. Two people have died. Why don't you just talk to the police?"

"I'm going to. I'm going to have a chat with Dave, the copper that I told you about at the golf club. But I need to tread carefully. If I'm completely wrong then I could be responsible for bringing a whole lot of trouble down on the Foundation's head."

Molly stifled a yawn and stood up.

"I'm going back to bed. I'm on an early shift at the Lodge tomorrow. And Jeremy, remember what I said. Be careful."

He watched as she left the room. The blue woolly dressing gown that she wore had been deliberately bought several sizes too big so that she could, as she expressed it, wrap herself in it. The effect was to make her look even smaller than she was. He was glad now that he hadn't told her about his fears of being followed. It had happened again today. He had just gone out for a brief walk, to get away from the report that he was trying to finish and he had been certain that somebody was watching him. When he turned around there was nobody there. It was a creepily odd feeling that had been difficult to shake off. If he was honest with himself, it had unnerved him.

43

THE MAN SAT and stared down at the floor, his head in his hands. He was missing something, he knew he was, something was stirring at the back of his mind. He could almost feel it pushing for release. He lifted his head again and stared up at the ceiling as though searching for inspiration. What was it? What had he done or not done? There was a piece of information floating tantalisingly before him, just out of grasp. He sat up straight and drew a deep breath to settle himself while he ran again through the events at the Mistletoe Hotel. They had arrived, all four of them within minutes of each other, and had the drink with Adam, even though none of them had wanted to. They had talked about the work of the Foundation, or at least Adam had, and they had answered his questions. But then he had started dropping hints that he wasn't entirely happy with the purchasing process of properties. Adam hadn't said anything specific but clearly he wasn't going to let the matter drop. He had smiled and nodded along with the others but that was when he had made the decision to use the poison.

He had bought it after the last trustees meeting, the one at which Adam had started asking awkward questions. He'd bought it really as a kind of surety. A way of feeling in control. There was something empowering about just having it in his possession. It hadn't been difficult to get hold of. In fact, it was funny really how remarkably easy it had been. The internet had surely been invented for people like him. There was almost nothing that you couldn't buy if you knew how. But he'd been careful, he had taken no chances. He had created a new email in a false name, used a work laptop, taken it into the park in town where the local authority had very thoughtfully provided free Wi-Fi, and placed the order from there. Then he had put the laptop in his brief case and taken a hammer to it when he got home. It had been easy to order a new one for the office. Nobody ever queried their purchase orders. Sometimes he thought that he could have ordered a nuclear warhead and it would simply have been processed without so much as a raised eyebrow.

The stuff itself he had arranged to have delivered to one of the properties that they'd recently purchased which was currently standing empty. When he had gone to collect it there had been all sorts of post addressed to previous tenants left lying on the hall floor. Mostly junk mail of the marketing variety and among it sat his own little packet. He had simply scooped up all the post, tucked his own into his inside pocket and deposited the rest in a neighbouring wheelie bin outside.

In the end, it had all been laughably simple. He had made the decision in a split second when everyone was taking a break before the Chairman's speech. There would never be a better opportunity. So many people were present and milling about that if suspicion was raised then it could have fallen on any one of them. He knew that he couldn't access the kitchen from the restaurant, he might be seen. But there must be more than one way in. Rising casually from his chair he had simply slipped outside and finding the fire door propped open, he had passed through to the kitchen. The room was empty. The kitchen staff were clearly taking a break. If one of them had come in, he would simply say that he wanted to say a personal thank you to them. The claret jug was standing, as he knew it would be, as it was every year, on a little silver tray. All right, he was taking a risk. Anybody could have seen him. But nobody did.

Annie had been different though. That had been much more hands on. Literally. Although he had still simply seized the moment. Taking a stroll in the grounds he had seen her through the kitchen window wrapping the claret jug. She had looked up and smirked at him, that horrible knowing smirk she deployed when she felt in control. He knew where the Foundation china and glass were kept and his guess was that she was heading down there to store the claret jug for the following year. He had looked around him. He was entirely alone except for a robin who had gazed at him with its sharp inquisitive eyes, head on one side, its fat little body perched precariously on little stick legs.

He had walked quickly towards the ice house, glad now of the boring tour that Dick had given each of them of the building and grounds when they had first joined the Foundation, and equally as glad of the snow which had begun to fall again and which would cover his foot tracks. Making his way through the tunnel, pausing only to pull on his gloves, he had emerged into the basement to see Annie's back as she busied herself among the shelves. Creeping up behind her he had clapped one hand over her mouth and thrown his other arm around her throat, pulling her backwards towards him. The old cow had more strength in her than he would have guessed and he had been momentarily thrown off guard by her resistance as she fought back. At one point she had almost got away from him by elbowing him in the ribs and stamping on his foot but he had pulled her back by her pinafore, ripping it in the process.

Looking down on her as she lay lifeless on the floor he had felt no pity. She had got what she deserved. He wasn't about to lose everything just because of some poxy old tea lady. And after all, it wasn't as if it was the first time. Even Adam hadn't been the first one. All of them had been spur of the moment decisions. In his heart he knew that he enjoyed it, that he revelled in the risk-taking. The wild recklessness of it, the feeling of omnipotence as he wiped out the life of a fellow human being. But, he assured himself, they had all been necessary. If they hadn't chosen to cross his path then they needn't have died. Really, when all was said and done, the choice had been theirs.

He stood up and stretched and suddenly the piece of jigsaw that he was looking for fell straight into place. Of course, Adam had a wife. He leaned forward and groaned. Why hadn't he thought of that? He knew that Adam had taken some of the Foundation's papers home with him, he had said as much over their drink at the Mistletoe hotel. It was reading through them that had raised his interest in the purchasing of properties. Men talked to their wives. What, if anything, had Adam said to his?

44

____

AUDREY PULLED open the front door and uttered the fatal words so beloved of television crime writers.

"Oh, it's you."

The man smiled at her.

"Dick asked one of us to drop round and I said that I'd call in on my way home. See how you're doing and if there's anything that you need and so on."

He paused for a moment as the unlikelihood of this suddenly struck him. But, he recollected, she didn't know Dick. She didn't know that the possibility of Dick considering anybody's welfare but his own was roughly nil.

Audrey nodded and beckoned him through to the sitting room. He looked around him. It was much as he might have expected. Tasteful. Some antique furniture, probably inherited. Adam and his wife weren't the sort of people who bought their own antiques. Thick rugs and an original fireplace. It was exactly the kind of room that confident, comfortable, affluent people inhabited.

"That's very thoughtful of you. Please sit down. Would you like a drink of something?"

"Oh no." He smiled again. "I don't want to put you to any trouble."

He turned as a strapping lad of about twenty entered the room. Sod it. That was another thing that he hadn't factored in. He was losing his touch. How was he going to find out if Audrey knew anything with that great hulk hanging around? The fewer witnesses to this conversation the better.

"This is my son, Oliver."

The lad smiled at him, a tight, wary smile as though assessing what interest this stranger might have in his mother. Although his father had only been dead for a short time, Oliver had already developed a son's instinct to ward off marauding males.

"He's come from the Foundation. To see if we're all right," she continued.

"And to collect any papers that Adam may have left," he added, seizing his opportunity. He looked at her, his eyes slightly narrowed. She gazed innocently back.

"Oh, yes. There were some. I gave them to Jeremy Goodman."

———

JEREMY WALKED SLOWLY along the beach, hands stuffed in his pockets. The incipient headache that had threatened to break out into a real hammering had subsided and he was starting to feel much better than he had earlier. He looked around him as he walked. He guessed that most people associated the sea side with the summer, the sun sparkling on the waves and children playing on the sand, couples walking hand in hand and eating ice cream. In the earlier part of the last century there would have probably been a Punch and Judy show here and perhaps a band playing on the pier. There might have been a photographer snapping the holiday makers and selling the images to them. When had they stopped plying their trade he wondered? He'd seen them in old films from the fifties but you didn't see them now. They'd probably gone out of business when cameras ceased to be a luxury item. Nowadays everybody that had a mobile phone had a camera. He paused for a moment and stared out across the broad grey expanse of the English channel. He couldn't paint or draw but he could appreciate the dramatic beauty of the seascape and the attraction that it held for artists like Turner.

Lifting his face he breathed in the cold air. He preferred it here in the winter. The summer season was enjoyable, especially when the weather was good. It was lovely to walk along the front and see families enjoying themselves, particularly the small children who patiently trotted back and forth to the sea to fill their buckets for the moats of the wonky sandcastles they had built. But there was a particular kind of melancholic desolate beauty to the scene at this time of year, a romantic yearning that even the most prosaic would find hard to resist. This afternoon was particularly cold and there were few people about, even the dog walkers seemed to have stayed at home.

He thought again about what he had discovered this morning. It hadn't taken him long and in truth, it didn't really take him much further. His research had only confirmed what he already knew or suspected. Setting up a limited company wasn't difficult. They could be, literally, bought off the shelf from one of the companies advertising those services. You didn't even need shareholders for a private limited company. Their main attraction seemed to be that the owners ceased to be personally liable for any debts that the company might accrue. What he had found of interest though, was that there was no footprint for Henry Holdings. He had conducted a thorough search on the internet. No reviews. No social media posts. No web site. Nothing. Not even an email address.

Surely, these days, every company who wanted success had a web site and used social media. Even corner shops and hamburger stands had a Facebook page. And they certainly courted reviews. Like many others, Jeremy was sick to death of being pestered with the inevitable 'how did we do?' every time goods were ordered or a parcel delivered. Unfortunately, the options given didn't include a tick box labelled 'total shite' when, after completing the purchase he'd been informed that there was a ten week wait for delivery. He'd noticed recently that even the supermarkets had started asking how his shopping trip had gone although they usually offered a little sweetener such as the chance to win a hundred pound voucher. But Henry Holdings left no such trace, which made it even more difficult to discover who was behind it.

There were four managers at Fireside House so in theory there were four potential suspects. Dick, he was certain, was not bright enough, or, to be fair, probably corrupt enough, to have been involved in any fraud. What Dick wanted was to turn up at the office, make himself feel important, and then go home again. Adam had said that he suspected that Dick was counting down the days to his retirement and that he almost certainly had a good pension coming, so it was unlikely that he would get involved in anything that would jeopardise that. Although, he reflected, he may well have been willing to turn a blind eye in order to protect his own position. But simply saying nothing or, more likely, not asking the right questions, didn't make a person guilty of a crime. Negligence, possibly, given the seniority of Dick's position, but probably not a criminal offence.

So that left Max, Nigel and Harry. Could they all be in it together? From what Jeremy had seen of them they were an unlikely alliance, but as far as Henry Holdings was concerned there was every possibility that they were working as a team. One way or another all the managers were involved in the general purchase of properties for the Foundation, therefore, even by default, they had all approved the purchases from Henry Holdings. But what about the murders? They couldn't all have done it, surely. Annie had been murdered in the basement. It was beyond the bounds of possibility that all three of them had crept down there and launched themselves at her. But, was it a plan that they had all agreed even though only one of them had carried it out? Surely in those circumstances the law would hold them equally liable?

He thought about what he knew of them. He had only met them three times. Once when he had attended the trustees meeting with Adam, once at the Mistletoe Hotel and then once when Adam had died and Dick had asked him in for a meeting. They had all been perfectly pleasant to him, but then why wouldn't they be? In fact being realistic, as chairman of the trustees, it was in their interest to keep on the right side of him. But when it came to their personal circumstances he didn't know the first thing about them. He didn't even know if they were married or how long they had worked for the Foundation. He toyed with the idea of getting Lettie to do a little research for him and then immediately abandoned it. If what he was beginning to suspect was true, asking questions might well place her in danger.

He glanced out across to the pier. It looked cold and abandoned, its metal structure stark against the failing light. It was getting really chilly now and it wouldn't be long before darkness fell. He had a sudden longing to be indoors, to be by the fire with Molly, Carlos and the cats and to forget all his worries, at least for this evening. He climbed back up to the main road and turned towards home. He didn't see the car until the last moment, head lamps on full beam as it bore down on him.

45

Jeremy pushed his fingers deeper into Aubrey's rich fur and held him close to his chest. Sometimes Aubrey reminded him of a teddy bear that he had as a child. There was the same plush like quality to his fur, the same warm comfort in holding him close. Aubrey relaxed against him and then pricked his ears, turning his head as the faint clack of the cat flap indicated that Vincent had just arrived home. Opposite Jeremy on the sofa Molly and Carlos sat quietly, staring at him. He looked at their faces and laughed suddenly.

"Don't look so tragic, the pair of you. It was probably just an accident. Somebody who had a bit too much to drink at the office party."

"That's not what you said when you came in." The accusatory note in Carlos's voice was unmistakeable. "You said that somebody tried to run you over."

"Well, I was just overreacting. Exaggerating. As I said, it was probably some driver who had one too many."

Jeremy bent over Aubrey's head and tickled his ear, unable to quite look Carlos in the eye. He had been, he had to admit, thoroughly shaken by the incident. Doubled over and gasping for breath, his heart pounding, he had raised his head just in time to see the red tail lights disappearing. It had been shocking to realise with such force that the space between life and death was paper thin. Here and then gone. A slip, a fall. A heart beat missed. A car out of control. Then the day that had started like any other, the normal mundane day, twisted and contorted and spun out of shape until reality was thrown into the air and the shrapnel that rained down was unrecognisable. For those concerned nothing would ever be the same again. But he wished now that he hadn't told Molly and Carlos. From the look on Molly's face, she wasn't about to let this go. She eyed him, head slightly to one side.

"Have you got Dave's number? The policeman that you know from the golf club?"

Jeremy nodded.

"Ring him."

"Molly, I really…"

"Ring him."

———

JEREMY WATCHED as Dave lifted the mug of coffee and took a long slow swallow. Their sitting room wasn't small by any means but Dave was one of those men who seemed to fill every space around him. Tall and broad with an accent that suggested the East Midlands, his habitually grumpy expression belied his kindly nature. He reached forward and took a biscuit from the plate that Molly was offering him.

"It's very good of you to drop round like this." Molly sat back in the chair opposite him. "Jeremy thinks I'm making a fuss."

Dave shook his head.

"Not at all. Anything and anyone connected with the Fireside Foundation is of interest to us right now."

Molly drew a deep breath and stared at him.

"So you really think that it was intended? That somebody deliberately tried to run Jeremy over?"

"I don't know." Dave looked solemn. "But I think that we should consider the possibility."

He replaced his mug on the little table and leaned towards Jeremy.

"So where was it, exactly?"

"Just on that stretch of road near the pier. I was walking along, thinking. I stepped out to cross the road and then this car suddenly seemed to come straight at me."

Dave nodded.

"When you say it came straight at you…"

"It was half on the pavement. It just sort of swerved off the road."

"I don't suppose you got the number or anything?"

Jeremy shook his head.

"No. I couldn't even tell you for sure what type of car it was. It was all so sudden and I was blinded by the headlights."

"Unfortunately, there are no cameras on that stretch of the road." Dave chewed on his bottom lip and looked thoughtful for a moment. "Any witnesses?"

"No. Not a soul. In fact I'd only been thinking minutes earlier how empty everywhere was. There wasn't another person in sight."

"Tell him, Jeremy," said Molly suddenly. "Tell him everything."

———

UP on the top level of the multi-storey car park the driver of the car pulled into a space and breathed in deeply. He'd been a bloody fool, he'd taken a risk too far. But he hadn't been able to resist it. It had happened almost before he knew what he was doing. Driving along the sea front, waiting at the lights, he had spotted Jeremy climb up to the main road from the beach and walk towards the kerb. Checking his rear view mirror that there was nobody behind him, he had driven slowly forward. At the last minute he had accelerated towards him, thrusting his foot down and gripping the steering wheel with both hands. The bastard had spotted him just in time, flinging himself out of the way and leaving him to bump clumsily along the kerb. Without waiting he had wrenched the wheels back onto the main road and driven off at speed.

He shouldn't have done it, he knew. It had been a last minute decision, like most of the others, but this one would have been just that bit too public. He had to admit though, the rush of adrenalin had been intoxicating.

46

MOLLY PUT ASIDE the crossword that she was working on and glanced across at Carlos. Sensing her gaze, he looked up from his football magazine and smiled glumly back at her. From outside the slushing sound of cars driving slowly through the snow filtered through.

"What is it, Carlos? You've barely spoken a word this evening. What's the matter?"

Carlos raised his shoulders in a slight shrug.

"Nothing."

Molly suppressed a sigh. Nothing. The catch-all teenage phrase. What are you doing? Nothing. What have you got there? Nothing. What's wrong? Nothing. Some lines of one of her A level texts filtered through the years. Nothing will come of nothing. Speak again. King Lear, if she recalled correctly. But that one hadn't ended well, either

"Is it Teddy?"

She spoke gently. She didn't want to force any confidences but he had been so low in spirits lately, so unlike his usual happy self. He had been looking forward to Christmas for weeks, he had made the Christmas cake back in November and bought festive sparkly collars for the cats. They had responded by simply staring at him while he fastened them around their necks and then stalked outside to remove and shred them. But now he seemed to have lost interest in everything. He had even left a packet of crisps half uneaten, which was unheard of. He looked back up at her, his eyes tortured, and nodded.

"Is she not answering your calls?"

He nodded again, keeping his mouth firmly closed. Molly realised suddenly that he was trying not to cry. She felt her own throat thicken. Carlos wasn't their natural son but he was a part of their family. She couldn't imagine life now without him. She sought for something to say but found nothing. The last time she had seen him look like this, so lost and bewildered, was when his mother died. Perhaps he might talk to Jeremy. She rose from the chair.

"Would you like to take a cup of hot chocolate up to Jeremy? I'm sure he could do with something, he's been up there for hours."

———

JEREMY TURNED AWAY from the computer screen as Carlos put his head around the door and thrust in a hand grasping a mug.

"Molly thought that you might want this."

From the mantelpiece where Aubrey and Vincent were parked like two bookends, they watched as Carlos advanced further into the room. Like Molly, they too were worried about him. Unlike Molly, they had been witness to some of the desperate and futile attempts by him to make contact with Teddy for the last two days. Last night had been particularly painful, when he had tried at least five times to no avail.

"She must know that I'm trying to talk to her. It'll come up as missed calls." He had stared mournfully at them as they had regarded him from the top of the chest of drawers. "I bet it's that Sebastian. I bet it bloody is."

And he had stood up, his face scarlet with rage and misery, and flung himself on the bed, burying his face in the pillow.

"If you're not doing anything in particular, you could proof-read this document for me," said Jeremy. "Just check that it makes sense."

"What is it?"

"It's just a few notes for my first meeting in the new year of the trustees. As the new chairman I think that I'm supposed to make some sort of opening address. I want to make it sound positive but it's a bit tricky, given everything that's happened."

Carlos nodded and sat down in the small armchair. He bent his head over the document that Jeremy handed to him. For several moments there was silence as he read down the page.

"Carlos," Jeremy hesitated and then ploughed on. "Is everything all right? You haven't seemed your normal self lately. Is everything all right at college? You've settled in okay and made friends and everything?"

"College is fine. It's good," he added. He put down the paper that he had been reading and smoothed across it with the palm of his hand. "Jeremy, you know, like, when you met Molly, was she your first girlfriend?"

Jeremy smiled.

"Good Lord, no. My first girlfriend was a little minx called Lizzie, and she led me a right dance, I can tell you!"

Carlos smiled. The first time, Aubrey realised with a sense of shock, that any of them had seen a smile on his face for days.

"Did she? What did she do?"

"Oh, turn up late. Or sometimes not at all. Or ring me to tell me that she wasn't sure that she really loved me and that we shouldn't see each other for a while."

Carlos stared at him, aghast.

"What did you do when she said that?"

"What any self-respecting teenage boy would do." Jeremy laughed suddenly. "Pleaded with her. And remember, that was in the days before mobile phones. Our phone was in the hall. Everybody could hear what you were saying if the sitting room door was open."

Aubrey watched with amusement as an appalled expression flitted across Carlos's face while he digested this. His mobile phone was as much a part of him as an arm or a leg. He used it for everything. Listening to music, watching films, looking up recipes. He rarely used a pen and paper apart from in lectures. He simply used the camera on his phone to record whatever he needed to. His phone was his lifeline to the world around him. But it was private. He could talk to whoever he pleased, wherever he pleased. There were never any listening ears other than his own and the person to whom he was speaking.

"So what happened in the end?" he asked finally.

"Do you know, Carlos, I'm not really sure. It just sort of fizzled out. I mean, there was no great bust up or anything. I started A levels and made new friends at college, and she started work so I suppose that we were on different paths then. I ran into her years later when I was visiting my parents. It was an odd feeling. At one time I thought that I would literally die of love for her. But when I saw her, there she was, an ordinary woman in her thirties with two small children in tow."

"Did she recognise you?"

"Yes, funnily enough she recognised me before I recognised her."

"So when did you meet Molly?"

"That was much later. After I finished university."

"Where did you meet?" asked Carlos, suddenly curious.

"At a bus stop. A bus was cancelled and we started talking. She'd just finished with her boyfriend and was feeling a bit glum." He laughed suddenly. "My guess was that she wouldn't stay unattached for very long so I didn't hang around. We walked back into town and I bought her a drink."

"Me and Teddy met at a bus stop, too. She showed me how to read the timetable."

"Is that what's wrong, Carlos? Is it Teddy?"

"She's not answering my calls." Carlos hung his head and spoke in a low voice as if to utter the words at greater volume would give them a reality that he didn't want to hear. "She's not posting anything either. It's like she's just sort of dropped into a great big hole." He raised his head again, suddenly alarmed. "You don't think she's dead, do you?"

"No, Carlos, I don't think she's dead. Perhaps she's got other things on her mind. Girls aren't like boys you know. They're different."

Aubrey and Vincent glanced at each other. Really? Talk about stating the bleedin' obvious.

"Perhaps you should just give her some space," Jeremy continued. "You know, let her ring you or WhatsApp or whatever it is you do when she's ready."

"Yes, but what if she's dead?" Carlos persisted.

Jeremy suppressed a grin.

"I would think that we might have heard, don't you? Anyway, get on with reading that document."

Carlos bent his head and then raised it again.

"I forgot to tell you."

"Forgot to tell me what?"

"You know that girl that works at the Mistletoe? Ella?"

"What about her?"

"Well, me and Rubble were talking to her in the common room the other day. And Rubble took out this translation thing from his pocket and started mucking about with it. It's a bit like a mobile," he explained. "It's got all these languages on it and it translates words."

"Right." Jeremy resisted the urge to tell him to get on with it. "A translation thing. Good. So what did Ella tell you?"

"Although," continued Carlos, ignoring Jeremy's question. "I don't know why Rubble wants a translation thing. He can barely read English."

"Carlos…" said Jeremy.

Carlos assumed a hurt expression.

"All right. Only I was going to tell you about this thing that Ella found."

Jeremy leaned towards him.

"What was it? What did Ella find?"

"That's what I was trying to tell you. This translation thing was in the lost property at the hotel. Guests and that often leave things behind and the staff put them in this special box thing for them to collect. If nobody collects them then eventually the staff can have them. Rubble says it's usually boring stuff like socks and pyjamas." He paused and looked thoughtful. "I mean, who would want somebody else's socks? Anyway, one of the things that was left was this translation thing and Rubble's dad said that he could have it until somebody claimed it."

Jeremy clasped his hands together and took a deep breath.

"So what did Ella find?"

"Well, Rubble was telling us about some of the mad things that people leave. Like once, there was this plastic dinosaur and…"

"Carlos…" This time the warning note in Jeremy's voice was unmistakeable.

"All right, I was getting to that bit. Ella said that the only thing that she had ever found was a cufflink. You know, like one of those things that posh blokes put in their shirts. She found it on the kitchen floor and handed it in."

"Does she remember when she found it?"

"She thinks it was day after the Foundation lunch. Only the

thing is, it couldn't have belonged to any of the kitchen staff because they would be wearing whites and you don't need cufflinks for those. Anyway, you're not supposed to wear jewellery or anything in the kitchen. In case it drops in the food," he added.

"Could the cufflink have belonged to the manager?"

Carlos shook his head.

"No, if it was his then he would have claimed it. He's the one who makes a list of everything that's handed in."

"What did this cufflink look like? Did Ella remember?"

"She said it was gold. And it had a pale blue stone set in it."

47

MAX DROVE HOME SLOWLY. He was in no hurry. Soon, Fireside House would be closed for ten days for the Christmas break but it wasn't a ten days that he was particularly looking forward to. Christmas had been different when his father was alive. Then he had driven over to the house on Christmas morning, sometimes with a girlfriend, sometimes not, armed with presents and looking forward to the glorious meal that his step-mother would prepare. Now he was going home to a house that would be either freezing cold or swelteringly hot, depending on what mood the old boot was in. Not for the first time, he found himself bitterly regretting agreeing to their current living arrangements. His old place had been small, true, but it had been cosy and at least he hadn't had to come home to never-ending battles which had become increasingly pointless on the basis that neither of them won.

The television would, he knew, be blaring, probably some game show that he never understood other than the requirement that the contestants should make a complete twat of themselves, and there would be nothing much to eat in the fridge. Only ready meals, which she seemed to live off nowadays. It was odd really, when he thought about it. She had been, he had to admit, a pretty good cook at one time. Almost at professional standard. Now it seemed to be about as much as she could do to drag herself over to the microwave. He glanced to his right at the bright lights of the supermarket. He might as well stop off and stock up with some fresh food. It would save him going out again later and he needed to get some cat food anyway.

He looked down at the cat basket on the passenger seat. Inside, Eric lay curled up asleep. Far from making a fuss, he had nodded off as soon as the engine started. Max gave him a warm affectionate smile. He had asked around at the Foundation if anybody knew if Eric had an owner but nobody had been able to give him any information. He didn't have a collar and when he had taken him back to the vet for a check-up after his injury, the vet didn't seem to think that he was micro-chipped either. He had taken Eric home for the night several times already, leaving him in his art studio shed with food and water, but now he'd decided that he would keep him at home permanently and move him into the house. Dick had already employed a new tea lady who was due to start in the new year. A tall spare woman with knobbly wrists and hands, she wore a hard thin-lipped expression that suggested she wouldn't have much truck with cats in the kitchen.

Events of recent weeks had taken their toll and he felt suddenly bone-achingly weary. The meeting this afternoon, the last of the year, had been fractious. Normally it was a jolly one, with each of them looking forward to the break. This year the mood had been one of barely concealed ill-temper, which had affected even Dick who normally managed to be emotionally absent for most of the time. They had each presented their annual report to him which had been met with a blank wall of indifference and none of them had been told by him what a splendid job they were doing. They might as well have been presenting last year's train timetable for all the interest he showed. Nobody had suggested breaking out the Foundation port.

Dick had clearly been keen to get away but the three of them had remained seated after he had bustled his way out, the papers that he clearly had no intention of reading tucked under his arm. They had sat and eyed each other suspiciously, all of them reluctant to speak but all of them equally reluctant to be the first to leave. The tension had crackled in the air until finally Harry had stood up and simply left the room, followed immediately after by Nigel. While the three of them could never have been described as friends, now they were openly hostile to each other. The sooner Henry Holdings died a death and they all went their separate ways the better. He had sat there on his own for several minutes, listening to the wind as it whistled around the side of the old house until eventually he had got up and left too.

———

ALL THE LIGHTS in the house were blazing as he pulled up. That bloody woman. She had recently taken to leaving every door open and every light on, irrespective of which room she was in. Unless she was in bed, in which case the house was left in total darkness so that when he arrived home he was left fumbling around trying to get the key in the lock. He suspected that she did it on purpose because she knew that it annoyed him. He placed the cat basket in the hall and hung his overcoat on the coat rack, and then turned as the sitting room door opened and his step-mother emerged. She looked as unappetising as ever although at least she had got dressed today.

She pointed a grubby finger at the cat basket.

"What's that?"

"An elephant," said Max and picking up the cat basket he pushed past her through to the kitchen. She followed him through, clearly spoiling for a fight.

"You can't keep that here."

She pressed her lips together and folded her arms. He looked at her, amused.

"And why is that, dear step-mother?"

"Because I said so."

She nodded as she spoke, triumphant that as far as she was concerned she was having the final word. Max tipped his head to one side. How long would it take, he wondered, for her to die? How much force would he have to exert around that scrawny neck to choke the life out of her? Nobody would miss her, that was for sure. She never went out. She'd lost touch with any friends that she'd ever had. But then, he reflected, he'd have the bother of getting rid of the body. Leaning over, he opened the cat basket and Eric marched out.

———

ACROSS ON THE other side of town, Nigel watched as his wife put yet more tinsel on the tree.

"It'll topple over if you load it down any more."

He spoke affectionately. Christmas with Ava was a joy. When the children had been at home she had always made it magical and now they had left she made it just as magical for him. The contrast between this warm tinsel-filled house and the Christmases of his childhood could not have been starker. Everything about those days had been cold, including the house. His only real enjoyment of Christmas had come from his primary school where the teachers painted snowflakes on the windows, they sang carols in assembly and every child was given a small tissue-wrapped gift. Once home, the atmosphere had been entirely different. Their tree, a small battered artificial one, was lugged out of the loft for its annual outing in the sitting room by his mother while his father studiously ignored her and stared at the television while she decorated it. On Christmas morning he invariably went to the pub and returned in a good mood, which generally lasted as long as it took the alcohol to wear off. Christmas dinner was eaten in silence, punctuated only by his father's criticisms of the cooking.

His mother, a silent ghost like figure had long since lost any fight that she ever had and simply acquiesced to her husband, as they all had. Taking the line of least resistance had always been the best option and one that he had learned early. His father's word had been law and his temper uncertain. He rarely raised a hand to any of them, but he didn't need to. An explosion of rage because one of them had made too much noise when eating or didn't answer quickly enough when he spoke to them left a thunderous cloud hanging over the whole house so that they had crept about like little blind mice, trying to keep out of his way. But the worse days by far had been the family days out.

He brooded silently on the memory of those trips. They always started well, with his father in high humour, checking the oil in the car and commenting on the likely mileage. By the time they arrived at the stately home or heritage museum that he had decided was essential for his son and daughter's education, he would already be simmering with rage because of some other driver refusing to give way or a new traffic system that he had failed to navigate successfully. Whatever it was, it was never his fault. By the time he had paid their entrance fees and started marching them through the building the atmosphere had been electric and they had all tiptoed along behind him, dreading that he would suddenly turn and demand an opinion on whatever it was that they were supposed to be appreciating. Nigel and his sister had longed for the day to end so that they could be in their own little rooms and away from him.

They had seriously discussed the option of killing him more than once. The first time he must have been aged about eleven, after which it became a fairly regular topic of discussion. He could see them now, he and his sister, heads bent together over the kitchen table, studiously doing their homework, one ear open for the sound of their father's key in the lock as he returned from work, and tensing themselves against whatever mood he might be in. The killing plan always took the same route. Neither of them was big enough to overpower him and the use of poison was too uncertain. The best way, they always agreed, was to shoot him and they spent many long hours discussing how to acquire a gun and which of them should learn how to use it. By the time he was seventeen the situation had resolved itself. His father had died of a heart attack. Watching television one evening he had made a strange noise and simply died. All three of them had turned their heads to look at him. None of them spoke. They waited fifteen minutes before they called an ambulance. He didn't feel guilty then and he didn't feel guilty now.

He watched as Ava stood back and regarded the tree. Whatever else happened, his plans for their future must not fall. Warm, loving and kind, Ava was the centre of his universe. He would do anything for her. Anything.

48

JEREMY STOOD PRETENDING to scan a shop window, very much aware that he was looking like the stereotype of the husband that has left the buying of any Christmas presents until the last minute. He smiled at the sudden memory of one of his uncles doing that very thing. They had been spending Christmas with his father's brother and his wife and so they had a ring side view of his aunt struggling to resist the temptation to plug in the electric whisk his uncle had given her as her Christmas present and shove it right up his arse. She had the last laugh though, she had hidden the paracetamol from him the next morning as he sat at the kitchen table, head in hands and his hangover dripping through his fingers. The last he had heard of them, they were tangled in divorce proceedings and frankly he wasn't surprised.

On the other side of the shop stood the Mistletoe Hotel. Edwardian in vintage, it was a red bricked imposing building much in demand by the local population for wedding receptions, anniversary dinners and the occasional wake. Decorated now with twinkling lights and a Christmas tree on the steps on either side of the entrance, it looked particularly inviting. He advanced towards it, and then hesitated for a moment, uncomfortably aware that he hadn't quite thought this thing through. His plan had been simply to turn up and somehow get a look in the lost property box. He couldn't try to claim anything as his own in case somebody else had already done so, which would make him look dodgy to say the least. Equally, if they gave it to him and then the real owner turned up he might be guilty of theft or something. After all, they presumably wouldn't just hand it over to him. They would surely, at the very least, take his details. There would probably be some form or something to fill in which he would have to sign. But he didn't really want to take it away anyway. He just wanted to get a look at it and then tell Dave. Well, he was here now. He'd manage it somehow.

The hotel reception looked warm and inviting, the decorations tasteful and the gentle music playing in the background discreet. When, he found himself suddenly wondering, did people stop putting out manger scenes at Christmas? His parents had one when he was little, a small set of plaster figures and a wooden stable. He had always enjoyed playing with it, although his parents had insisted that it was not a toy. But he had liked the little shepherds grouped around the crib and the way his father always put the three kings out later. When he had asked why, he had been informed that they hadn't arrived yet. He couldn't remember now the last time he had seen such a nativity set. He wondered if it was even still possible to buy them. He was called back to the present by the sound of the receptionist's voice.

She looked at him, her face pleasant but impassive while he stumbled out his story.

"A cufflink you say? Well, I can look in the cupboard for you. When did you say that you lost it?"

"I'm not quite sure. Actually," he said suddenly, as inspiration came to him, "It's not mine. It belongs to a friend of mine. He thought that he must have lost it here before he went back home. To Wales," he added as his inner voice told him to shut up talking, to resist the temptation to keep elaborating. "I said I'd call in and check when I was passing."

The woman nodded, clearly uninterested in the rapidly invented back story. He watched as she disappeared through a door marked 'private' and then re-appeared carrying a large plastic crate. She placed it on the desk between them and opened it. Inside were a number of small packages, each labelled with a date and a name.

"You're welcome to look through these," she said, tipping them out carefully and spreading them with her fingers. "What's your friend's name? Was he a guest here?"

Jeremy swallowed and bent over the small packages.

"Er, no. He didn't actually stay here. He just stopped in for a drink. He'd been working away and was on his way home. He thinks that he must have lost the cufflink here as he was sure he was wearing it when he came in. The cufflinks have special sentimental value to him. His wife bought them on their first wedding anniversary."

He bit his lip. He was doing it again. Lying didn't come naturally to him and on the few occasions he had been reduced to doing it, he nearly always went too far out of panic. The classic example was when, aged eleven, he had conducted a chemistry experiment in his bedroom which had gone wrong. The result had been an unsightly scorch mark on his bedroom carpet and a distinct odour of burning, the smell of which had reached the kitchen where his mother was preparing dinner. His tale that the experiment had actually been part of a school project which had been set for them by the chemistry teacher had been met with a dubious look. When his mother called his bluff and had said that she would complain to the school about it, he had tearfully told her that the teacher in question was under a lot of stress and that his wife had left him with their seven children, one of whom was seriously ill in hospital. His mother had responded with a very stern look and demanded the return of the box of kitchen matches that he was still holding.

He stared down now at the contents of the box and reached towards the little package with the name Ella and the word 'kitchen' attached to it. He swallowed. Visitors to the hotel didn't normally stray through to the kitchen. How would he explain to the receptionist that his imaginary friend had lost his cuff link in there? Keeping his eyes firmly down and praying that she wouldn't ask, he read the date on the label. It matched the day after the Foundation lunch. He opened the package and held the gold cufflink for a moment in the palm of his hand, the gentle gleam of the blue stone just caught the light.

"Is it the right one?" The receptionist peered down, mildly curious.

"Er, I'm not really sure. He didn't actually describe it. He just said it was gold."

"Why don't you take a photograph of it and text it to your friend? Then he can tell you if it's his. Although," the receptionist added before turning back to her computer screen, "I think it must be. I can't recall ever having had a cufflink handed in before. People don't wear them so much now, do they?"

Jeremy beamed at her and reached into his pocket for his phone. Even if the owner came back and claimed it, he now had a picture of it and a record of when and where it was found.

49

AUBREY AND VINCENT emerged back through the tunnel and looked at each other. Outside, darkness had fallen and Fireside House was silent. The light from the reception area, which was always kept on, glimmered faintly though the fan light of the door.

"He's definitely not in the house, Vin. We've looked everywhere."

"What if he's in one of the rooms with the door closed?"

Aubrey shook his head.

"No. We called him. He would have heard us and answered."

"Unless he's ill," said Vincent.

They both fell silent. They hadn't seen Eric for nearly three days now and were starting to feel anxious about him.

"He said that he lives in other places, too. Perhaps he's at one of his other homes?"

The tone of hope in Aubrey's voice was unmistakeable. In the short time that they had known him, he and Vincent had grown fond of Eric. They were used to his long silences because whenever he did speak it was usually something worth saying. Aubrey hugged hope to himself that right now Eric was curled up in front of the fire at one of his other addresses. They crept out from the ice house and both instinctively looked towards the road. They couldn't see it from where they were but they could hear it. Traffic there was never light at the best of times and it was always a threat to cats and other small creatures who frequently ended up under the wheels of a driver who hadn't seen them until it was too late.

"Well," said Vincent. "I expect he'll turn up."

Aubrey nodded. He wasn't so sure. He was beginning to get a bad feeling about this. He watched as Vincent lifted his handsome face towards the stars that clustered in the dark sky. Vincent was his best mate and he cared for him as much as he cared for Molly, Jeremy and Carlos, but sometimes he had the feeling that he didn't know him at all. Where, for instance, did he keep disappearing to? He opened his mouth to speak and then closed it again. If Vincent didn't want to tell him, then he shouldn't ask. He stiffened suddenly at the sound of a car turning into the little carpark. There shouldn't be anybody here at this time. All the workers had gone home hours ago. It was after midnight, which was why he and Vincent had chosen this time to look for Eric. He nudged Vincent and they watched, eyes gleaming, as a shadowy figure walked softly round the side of the house and approached the front door.

The man punched in the code and, giving a quick glance over his shoulder, let himself in. This was madness. He knew it. But once the thought had formed in his mind he couldn't shake it loose again. He knew that he would have no peace until he'd checked. He had obviously noticed that the cufflink was missing before tonight but after that he hadn't really thought about it again. He had been careless with fastening cuff links before and it wasn't the first time that he had lost one. But tonight he had woken from a confused dream in which he had been searching for something that he couldn't find and a ghastly thought had snaked its insidious way into his mind and slithered across his brain until it was impossible to shake it out again. What if the missing cuff link was somewhere that it didn't ought to be?

He couldn't remember the last time he had worn the cufflinks but they were quite new, so that must mean that the missing one had disappeared recently. What if he had been wearing them the day he had killed Annie and it had fallen out in the struggle? She had kicked and fought. It might easily have dropped to the ground. But surely the police would have found it? If they had then presumably he would have known about it by now. He was worrying about nothing, surely. The missing cuff link was probably under his bed or caught up in the sleeve of a jacket or something. It would turn up eventually. It was almost certainly somewhere in the house. Anyway, he could have lost it in the basement when he was down there for a quite innocent purpose. But none of the managers went down there, for innocent purposes or otherwise.

He had pushed it from his mind and tried to settle himself back to sleep, punching his pillow and turning it over in an effort to get comfortable, but the notion persisted. If only he could remember for sure the last time that he had been wearing them. The memory of Annie and her surprisingly solid little body as he choked the life out of it persisted. She had grabbed at his arm as she sank down, he was sure. The cufflink may have dropped out and rolled under one of the shelves where it had got caught in the dust. It might easily have been missed by the people searching. And if it was there, it would sit like a little ticking time bomb just waiting to explode. He checked himself. He wasn't the only man at the Foundation who routinely wore cufflinks. As long as he got rid of the other one, they couldn't identify it as his.

He had sat up again. It was no good. He knew that he would have to go and look. Why take chances? But it would be better not to be seen entering the basement during office hours, somebody might easily wonder what he was doing. Pulling on his jeans and a sweatshirt, he had reached across to the small leather box that stood on top of a chest of drawers. Rummaging through it, he pulled out the mate of the cufflink that he had lost. He had pushed it down into his jeans pocket and grabbed his car keys. If he didn't find the other cuff link, he would get rid of this one on the way home. Just to be on the safe side. Drop it off the end of the pier from where it would sink to the bottom of the English Channel.

HE CREPT across to the basement and started to tiptoe down the steps. He paused and peered down into the gloom. He had nothing to worry about, he had his story ready. If, on a million to one chance, anybody should enter the building, he would simply say that he had lost his wallet and thought that it might be in his office, he'd heard a noise in the basement and gone down to check. He reached the bottom and flicked on the lights. At the entrance to the tunnel, in the shadow, two cats sat watching him.

Aubrey turned to Vincent.

"What's he doing?"

"Nothing that's any good, that's for sure Aubsie."

Aubrey nodded. Vincent was right. The man was clearly up to no good. Why else would he be creeping about at night? They both knew who he was. He worked at the Foundation. They had seen him several times in the grounds. They watched as, using his phone as a torch, he began searching in the dark space beneath the shelving, running his hand along the floor and grunting with the effort of crouching so low. At one point he straightened up and stood for a moment with his hand pressed into the small of his back before dropping back down again and continuing the search.

50

Molly turned from the vegetables that she had been chopping as Carlos came into the kitchen.

"How was your last day?" she asked.

Carlos pulled out a chair and sat down at the table.

"All right. The lecturers were all going to the refectory for a pi…" he paused and then continued. "Drink, so they chucked everybody out at midday. We went to the King George to celebrate the end of term."

Molly raised her eyebrows. The King George, while not the worst public house on the south coast, did have a reputation for attracting a certain type of customer. Usually the sort that had trouble written all over them. She and Jeremy had only been in there once and had left after one drink. Nothing had actually happened but the atmosphere had been unsettling and they had decamped to a more sedate establishment further down the road. To be fair though, the King George probably did have attractions for teenaged boys, not least of which would be not asking their age.

"They don't ask for ID," Carlos said as if reading her thoughts, and added, "Rubble got drunk."

Molly nodded, relieved. Not that Rubble had got drunk, but that Carlos hadn't. She knew from her own sixth form days how silly youngsters could be, especially when they were hyped up by the end of term, and especially when it was Christmas. She remembered very well one girl bringing in a large cocktail shaker in which she had mixed a number of alcoholic drinks. They had all drunk from it, with the result that the rest of the day had passed in something of a haze, with one or two of them quietly throwing up in the cloakroom and having to be helped out to the school bus afterwards. At least Carlos had arrived home in pretty much the same state he had been in when he left this morning.

"How did Rubble get home?"

"We walked him back. Luckily his mum and dad were out. Molly," he hesitated and then ploughed on. "There's this girl at college. Ella."

"The one that works at the Mistletoe Hotel? Jeremy told me about her. She's on the same course as you, isn't she?"

Carlos nodded.

"Well, I think that she sort of likes me." He reddened slightly. "I mean, like, she always sort of seems to be there."

"Well, that's not so surprising is it, if she's on the same course as you?"

"But she keeps talking to me. And today, at the pub, she kept saying that there should be mistletoe and that and everybody laughed."

Molly smiled.

"Do you know what the English Christmas tradition for mistletoe is?"

"No. What?"

"People kiss under it."

Carlos looked appalled.

"What? Like right in front of everybody and that?"

"Yes, Carlos. Right in front of everybody and that." She

smiled again and leaned forward to ruffle his hair. "Don't look so horrified."

"The thing is, Molly, I like Ella. She's really nice. She's, like, a good laugh and all that. But I don't like her in that way." He stumbled slightly over his words. "I mean, not like a girlfriend. Do you know what I mean?"

Molly nodded. She did know what he meant. In fact the night she had met Jeremy she had just finished with her boyfriend because, as Carlos had so eloquently expressed it, she didn't really like him in that way.

They both turned as the letterbox rattled.

"I'll go," said Carlos.

Molly went back to the vegetables. Carlos was turning into a very good-looking boy. Ella wouldn't be the only one to have her head turned. But all Carlos wanted was Teddy and right now Teddy seemed to have disappeared from the face of the earth. She sighed. Teddy had seemed such a nice girl. Not the sort to be deliberately cruel. Surely, if she didn't want to see Carlos again she would have told him, not just left him hanging about like this. She had half thought about ringing Teddy's parents to enquire if everything was all right but had eventually decided against it. It smacked a bit too much of interfering and besides which, Carlos was going to have to learn how to navigate his own way in life. She and Jeremy couldn't shield him forever. And they certainly couldn't shield him from having his heart broken.

She looked up again as Carlos returned carrying the post, his long fingers flicking through the envelopes.

"Anything interesting?"

"It looks like mostly Christmas cards."

"Do you want to open them?"

She turned back to the vegetables as he sat down at the table again and began ripping open the envelopes.

"Molly, Molly."

Carlos sounded breathless, his voice half choked. Alarmed, Molly dropped the vegetable knife and span round. Carlos looked up at her, his eyes gleaming. In his hand he was holding a postcard, on the front of which pictured a romantic looking mountain at sunset.

"It's from Teddy," he breathed. "She's doing this camping thing up a mountain and she can't get a signal on her phone where they're staying. She says that she'll call as soon as she gets back."

"Ello, 'ello, 'ello, what's going on 'ere then?"

Jeremy strolled into the kitchen and dropped the wallet folder that Audrey had given him onto the table.

"Carlos has had a postcard from Teddy. She's on a camping trip or something."

Jeremy sat down at the table and smiled at Carlos.

"Excellent." He turned to Molly. "I thought I'd come down here and join you two. I was getting a bit lonely up there."

He opened the wallet folder as he spoke and began spreading the contents in front of him. Molly cast her eyes upward.

"Jeremy, I think that you should leave all that alone now. You've done what you can. Let the police do their job."

Jeremy opened his mouth to reply and then closed it again. She was right, of course. But somehow, somewhere at the back of his mind, he couldn't help thinking that if he searched a bit harder, looked a little more closely, he just might find the thing that he was looking for. The problem was of course that he didn't know what that thing was. He picked up Adam's notebook again and flicked through it. He'd been through it so many times now that he knew it practically word for word. In fact, he'd made notes on the notes. He put it back down again and picked up a Foundation newsletter. There was Dick, looking serious and important in his immaculate grey suit, seated at his imposing desk, eyes cast down, pretending to study what presumably the reader was supposed to think was an important document. It was, he thought, just as likely to be copy of the Beano. He sighed. The sooner that Dick retired the better.

He dropped the newsletter back on the table and pulled the next one towards him. It was a real archive piece, produced he guessed, in the nineteen seventies. The main photograph showed the Foundation staff standing by a Christmas tree. He smiled to himself. The woman to the left of the picture was wearing exactly the sort of dress that his mother used to wear. Knee length crimplene with a neat little belt. She even had the same sort of hair style. Softly waved and flicking slightly at the ends. He picked it up and half turned to Molly to show her when his eye was caught by the newsletter beneath it. This one was much more recent. He glanced to the top of the page. It had been produced just three months ago. The main picture in this one showed one of the managers handing over a key to a new tenant. And clearly showing in the cuff of his shirt as he shook hands was a gold cufflink set with a pale blue stone.

51

———————

JEREMY LEANED on the golf club bar and took a long gulp from his pint of beer. The lunch-time rush had gone and the bar was half-empty. The Christmas lights and decorations were up and, Arnold, the barman, was wearing a Santa hat with a bit of tinsel wound around it and a fake white beard. Being a tall thin man of a naturally lugubrious expression, Jeremy thought that it made him look rather sinister. Just as well that children weren't allowed in the bar, they'd be carrying them out screaming. Next to him Carlos sipped at his half of lager. He had been initially reluctant to buy it for him but then he recalled a vague memory of reading somewhere that youths of sixteen or seventeen could drink alcohol with a meal provided that it was bought by an adult. Well, the golf club was a private members club and it did serve food. Anyway, it was Christmas and he doubted that the golf club would be at the top of the list for police raids.

He glanced sideways at him. It had been a good idea to get Carlos out of the house this afternoon. He had been excitable and on edge ever since receiving Teddy's postcard and today seemed like as good a time as any to give him his first golf lesson. On the whole, it had been rather successful. Jeremy hadn't really been surprised. Carlos had all the makings of a good golfer. He was tall and lean and had a natural swing and a good eye. It would, he thought, be an idea to build these sessions into their weekly routine. Apart from anything else, he thought, casting a rueful glance down at his stomach, it would give him some much-needed exercise as well.

He looked up as Dave strolled in and joined them at the bar.

"The usual?"

Dave nodded.

"Shall we grab a table?"

Holding their drinks, the two men and Carlos made their way towards a table in the corner and sat down. Carlos straightened his shoulders and assumed a serious expression, flattered to be in the company of grown men. Although given what he'd learned of his father, Jeremy thought, he probably hadn't had much practice.

"I called round at your place as soon as I came off duty." Dave took a sip from his pint. "Molly said that you were here. I thought that you'd want to know."

Jeremy put his pint down.

"Why? What's happened?"

"We took him in a couple of hours ago. He came quietly but he's not saying anything. He just sat back and called his solicitor."

"Was it the cufflink?" Carlos, his tone eager, leaned forward.

"Pretty much," said Dave. "We knew that, certainly as far as Annie was concerned, everybody who was in Fireside House that day was a suspect, given that there were no visitors and no strangers reported hanging about and it would have been too much of a coincidence not to have linked her death with Adam's. The cufflink at least gave us something to make a start with."

"Isn't it all a bit, you know, circulation?" asked Carlos.

"Circulation?" Dave looked puzzled.

"Circumstantial," Jeremy translated. Years of working with teenagers had developed his skill at interpreting down to a fine art. He considered his best effort to be the day he had been marking some homework and had finally managed to translate 'I was groping with my wok' to 'I was working with my group'. The boy who had written it, he recalled, had been a small blond wiry lad who, in spite of his inability to grapple successfully with the English language, had been a gifted musician. Jeremy had heard him once playing on the battered old upright piano that stood in the corner of the long defunct music room at Sir Frank Wainwright's. He had looked embarrassed when Jeremy had put his head round the door to find out where the music was coming from and had stood up and quickly shut the lid of the piano, almost certainly anticipating that he was going to get a bollocking for being in there. Instead, Jeremy had simply sat down and asked him to continue. He remembered that afternoon well. It had been a little oasis of calm and beauty, a unique occurrence at Sir Frank's. He wondered where the boy was now. By rights he should have been playing for a symphony orchestra. Probably he was working for the minimum wage in one of the huge warehouses that banked the ring road. Just like Carlos might have been if he and Molly hadn't fostered him.

"Well, yes," Dave conceded. "It is circumstantial. But there's no doubt about the fact that the cufflink was found on the kitchen floor of the Mistletoe Hotel the day after the Foundation Christmas lunch, and that it looks very much like it belonged to him. As evidenced by the picture in the newsletter. And also, he had no business being in the kitchen."

"He could just say that the cufflink wasn't his," said

Carlos. "That loads of people might have had cufflinks like that."

"He could," admitted Dave. "But we took it to a jeweller in town who confirmed that it would have cost a pretty penny so probably not owned by loads of people. But I take your point. Anyway, it's a start. It's given us a reason to take him in for questioning. We'll just have to keep digging until we get some more. We're going to do another sweep around Fireside House tomorrow. If we can place him in the basement somehow, it will help."

"How long can you keep him," asked Jeremy.

"Twenty-four hours and then we have to either charge or release him. Although," he added, "we can apply for an extension if the charge is likely to be a serious one, which this is."

"What did you find out about Henry Holdings?" asked Jeremy. "Did you get anything there?"

Dave looked glum.

"Not really. Going through the transactions, they're genuine enough. There is a company called Henry Holdings and they did sell property to the Foundation, albeit at vastly inflated prices but that in itself isn't a crime. People pay over the odds for things all the time. Caveat emptor and all that."

Carlos looked interested. More new words to impress Teddy with.

"Cave what?" he asked.

"Caveat emptor," said Jeremy. "It means buyer beware."

Carlos nodded. He wasn't sure how he was going to work that one into a conversation but he'd give it his best shot.

"Anyway," continued Dave, "all the paper work is in order. They were legitimate sales. If we're lucky we might be able to get some kind of deception or fraud charge to stick. But that's assuming that we can find someone to stick it to. We can't seem to unearth who's behind the company."

"What about the purchase money from the properties? It must have been paid somewhere." Jeremy sounded puzzled. "Can't you track it through bank accounts or something?"

"We tried that. The money was siphoned off from the Henry Holdings account into the accounts of people who really exist. Foundation tenants who knew nothing about it."

"Can you just do that?" asked Carlos. "I mean just sort of open an account in somebody else's name?"

"It's easier than you might think," said Dave. "It's not like the old days when you had to actually go to the bank and do things in person. If I remember correctly, you had to have references as well. But now days lots of this stuff is done online. And all the details of the tenants were on file at the Foundation. Dates of birth, national insurance numbers, the lot."

Jeremy looked thoughtful.

"Right. So where did the money go after that?"

Dave grimaced.

"Into a range of off-shore investment accounts about which the tenants…"

"Knew nothing," Jeremy finished for him. "Can you get anything there?"

"We'll try but it's not as easy as you might imagine. These accounts are held off-shore for a reason."

"What about the directors of Henry Holdings?" Jeremy persisted. "They must be listed somewhere."

"Again, they're apparently tenants of the Foundation. We've interviewed them, of course. But none of them seem to know anything about it. And I believe them."

"What happens now then? I mean, it's obvious that someone at the Foundation is behind Henry Holdings."

"The problem is, finding out who that someone is. The details on tenants are held on file. Pretty much anybody at

Fireside House has access to them. So, in theory, everybody who works there is a suspect."

Jeremy looked appalled.

"Not the office staff, surely? They didn't have a say in which properties were purchased."

Dave shrugged.

"One or more of them could have been an accomplice. Just because they're nice women, it doesn't mean that they're nice women." He paused. "If you see what I mean."

Jeremy nodded. It was true. Beth, the erstwhile school secretary who had fleeced the school of thousands, had been a nice woman.

"Anyway," Dave continued, "we'll obviously get the IT forensics onto Henry Holdings. Other than that we'll have to hope that either he'll crack, which I doubt, or some DNA will turn up somewhere where he shouldn't have been. Interestingly, he was already in our system."

Jeremy looked astonished.

"No! What for?"

"Handling stolen goods. Received a suspended sentence when he was fifteen. Couldn't believe it when I saw it. There it was in black and white. Harry Field.

52

———————

Harry sat in the gloomy little interview room and stared at the wall on which somebody had scribbled the letters acab. He smiled suddenly. When he was a teenager he and another lad had been stopped by the police on suspicion. On suspicion of what they hadn't clarified. When the other boy had been asked why he had the letters acab tattooed on his forearm the lad had simply replied that it was to remind him. Of what, the copper had asked. And with an entirely straight face and an angelic smile the lad had said, "always carry a bible." He wondered what had happened to that boy. Probably a cabinet minister by now.

He leaned back and stretched, clasping his hands behind his head. He glanced across at the uniformed officer sat in the corner, his face impassive. Presumably he was there to guard him. From what? What did they think he was going to do? Start running amok through the police station? Apart from anything else, he didn't have the energy. He sat forward again, flicked a speck of cotton from his trouser leg, and pinned his elbows to the table. So far he'd said nothing and until his solicitor arrived he would continue to say nothing. It was bloody bad luck about the cufflink though. His instinct had told him that he needed to find it and his instinct had been right. He had just been looking in the wrong place.

Was it, he wondered, possible to extract DNA from gold? Probably. They could get it from almost everything else. Anyway, if they did, all he would have to do was to come up with a plausible story as to why he was in the hotel kitchen on that day. Or why somebody else had picked the cufflink up and put it in the kitchen. They wouldn't get his DNA from anything else in there, he was certain of that. He'd touched nothing, just poured the powder into the claret jug, making sure that he kept his hands free from any surface. He had even had the presence of mind to wrap his hand in his handkerchief, just in case. The basement was another matter, though. He might well have left some trace down there when he was searching for the cuff link. But just because the managers generally didn't go down there, it didn't mean that they never went down there. Anyway, he'd think of something. Some reason why he had found it necessary to visit the basement. Coming up with plausible stories was a thing that he'd been doing all his life. It was how he made his living. All he had to do was keep his cool, which was something else that he'd been doing all his life.

Through the open door he watched as a drunken miscreant was hauled off to a cell by two burly police officers, the unmistakeable stench of urine and stale sweat wafting through as they dragged him past. The smell, redolent of underpasses and public lavatories in town centres, pulled the unwelcome image of his mother to mind. The last time that he had seen her, lying on her stained and reeking bed, floated in front of him. That Christmas night the sound of her drunken snoring had reverberated through the whole of the flat and he had lain in his little bed silently hating her. Christmas had been no different to any other. She had got up late with a hangover and then given them some cheap toys which they were too old for and which looked distinctly second-hand. After drinking half a bottle of cheap sherry, she had made her usual marginal effort at cooking Christmas dinner which had consisted of dried out chicken, lukewarm gravy and burnt potatoes, and then she had gone out to the pub. He and his brother and sister had huddled together on the sofa watching television and eating sweets. She had returned several hours later, barely able to stand, and collapsed on her bed.

It hadn't been difficult to creep into her room and locate the bottle of cheap vodka that she always kept by her side. She had barely stirred when he had pinched her nostrils together, forced her mouth open and poured the vodka down her throat. She was heavy but she was weak. All her flesh was broken-veined blubber with no strength behind it. At one point she had struggled to sit up, half-choking, coughing and spluttering, but he had continued holding her down by one shoulder and pushing the neck of the bottle further into her mouth until it had all gone. Then he had stood and watched and waited for her to die. He had decided that if necessary, he would place a pillow over her face but he hadn't needed to. She had simply stopped breathing.

He knew that very few questions would be asked. She was well-known both to the police and to the local surgery and hospital where she had been taken on a number of occasions having been found lying in the street or, as on one memorable occasion, kicking the wheels and hammering on the windscreen of a stationary car while the terrified driver sat inside. All he had to do that night was keep it simple. And he had. After carefully arranging the now empty vodka bottle in her hand, he had telephoned for an ambulance, saying that he had discovered his mother in that condition and that he couldn't waken her. The ambulance had arrived and taken her away. There had been little interest. Nobody had asked why he had gone into her room in the first place. She had been a nuisance when she was alive and the authorities were glad to see the back of her. Her funeral had been a simple local authority affair which had been arranged by a local government officer with responsibility for such matters. His father was in prison again but wouldn't have been interested even if he hadn't been. Harry had never felt guilty and he didn't feel guilty now. And neither did he feel guilty about Adam or Annie. They had threatened him and it had been necessary to get rid of them. It was their own fault. All right, he would admit that he got a certain thrill out of it, as much for not being caught as the actual act, although that looked as though it was about to backfire, but he wasn't mad. He wasn't a complete lunatic, not like Bruce.

He half-smiled at the memory of Bruce. He had been the minder at the house where he lived with the women. Almost as wide as he was tall, with a number of teeth missing and an interesting scar that meandered down the left side of his face, he was exactly the kind of person that you wouldn't want to run into on a dark night. Or any night. Where Bruce had been recruited from, nobody knew. He had simply turned up one day and announced that henceforth he was responsible for security. The women hadn't minded. They sometimes had difficult punters and a bit of muscle around the place wouldn't do any harm. Bruce had drunk tea with Harry sometimes in the kitchen, poring over a tabloid that he could barely read and pausing occasionally to instruct Harry in the best methods of torture. He had described the gruesome details as simply and as casually as explaining how to mow a lawn. The last Harry had heard of him he had begun to identify as female, renamed himself Lena, and had opened a tea shop in the north of England.

He pulled his mobile out of his pocket and began scrolling through it. Nothing of any interest. He had half-wondered if

Max would crack and call him. Nigel wouldn't, he knew, but Max might. If he did, he would just not accept the call. Anyway, those two would be safe as long as they kept their mouths shut. They had covered their tracks as far as humanly possible and he had kept an absolute poker face when the police had asked him about Henry Holdings. He leaned back and stretched again. If this went to trial, whether he was found guilty or not, it would be the end of his dream of starting his own agency. Not many clients would willingly sign up with somebody who had stood trial for murder. He realised suddenly that he didn't care very much. If he was found guilty then he would be a model prisoner and serve his time. The money would still be there. If he served ten years he still wouldn't be quite sixty. He could go abroad and start a new life. Buy a yacht and sail the world. Or maybe, he grinned suddenly, stay in England. Live in a village. Go to church and live the life of a model parishioner.

53

Nigel nibbled gently on the side of his thumb, his other hand tapping lightly on his desk. Opposite him sat Max, his face impassive while he thought about the date he had later with Diana, the receptionist. He had asked her on an impulse, having caught a drift of her exquisite perfume as he passed her desk. He had found himself stumbling over the words as he suddenly wondered if this would constitute some form of harassment. That would be all he needed now, a tribunal for inappropriate behaviour. To his astonishment she had smiled what could only be interpreted as a smile of encouragement and said that she would be delighted to have dinner with him. Would she, he found himself wondering, be interested in living with an artist on an island? With Eric, of course.

Outside, the clear true note of the robin rang out in the winter air, oblivious to the drama that was being played inside the building. From downstairs the gentle thud and knock sound of searching rose through the open door of the basement as police undertook a further sweep for evidence. Dick, white-faced and strained, had left them shortly after they had all witnessed Harry being escorted from the building and into a waiting police car. With his usual baseball bat approach for understanding people, Dick had decreed that the subject was not to be discussed around the offices or indeed anywhere else. He had sent all the women home to start their Christmas break early and then shut himself in his office. His ill-temper pulsated through the building.

"This doesn't change anything," said Nigel.

"It does for Harry," Max replied, pulling himself back from thoughts of Diana and her pretty little pearl-nailed fingers and her soft wavy hair. "What will we do if he starts talking about Henry Holdings?"

"He won't."

Max stared at him.

"How do you know that?"

Nigel tipped his head to one side.

"Think about it. It's obvious. If he talks now, not only will he be in prison but he'll be in prison with no money. In the meantime, nothing changes. The money is safe, trust me. As far as you and I are concerned, the Foundation bought properties from Henry Holdings in good faith. So we just leave everything as it is, bide our time, and then we make a strategic exit."

"And what about Dick?"

"What about him?"

"Now the police are asking questions about Henry Holdings, he's going to start asking his own questions."

Nigel laughed suddenly.

"You think so? You don't seriously think that Dick is going to do anything that might jeopardise his own position? If he starts asking questions, he might find out things that he didn't want to know. He hasn't got long to go now before he gets his very juicy pension. My confident prediction is that he will suddenly develop a medical condition that requires complete rest and thus an early retirement.

"What about the trustees?"

"The trustees, if they've got any sense, will draw a line under it all."

"But the police are going to want to know why Harry killed Adam and Annie." Max persisted. "I mean, what reason is he going to give? That they just got on his nerves or something? I'm still not sure myself," he added, "why he killed Annie."

"Max, you heard her yourself that day when she brought the coffee into the meeting. She was almost boasting that she knew something."

"Do you think that she did?"

Nigel shook his head.

"I doubt it. Anyway, as far as Harry is concerned, he doesn't have to say anything. If he's got any sense, he'll just plead guilty and then he doesn't have to answer any questions at all. It depends on how much they've got on him. Also, a guilty plea will count in his favour."

Max nodded.

"I suppose so." He paused. "You knew it was him, didn't you?"

"Didn't you?"

54

AUBREY FINISHED the last scraps of food in his bowl and looked up as Jeremy came through the back door, stamping the snow from his shoes and rubbing his hands together. He wandered over to him, tail erect, and then turned as the cat flap went and Vincent made his usual elegant entrance, paws first followed by the rest of his sleek dark body. Unlike Aubrey, who usually managed it by pushing and shoving and then landing on the mat with a faint air of surprise. He stared at his friend. Funny how whenever Jeremy came home, Vincent arrived back shortly after. He'd never noticed it before.

"All right, Vin?"

Vincent nodded and headed towards his food bowl.

"Been anywhere nice?"

"Just around."

Aubrey grinned to himself. Of course. That was where Vincent went when he mysteriously disappeared. He was following Jeremy. He was checking that he was all right. The disappearance of Vincent's previous owners had affected him more deeply than he had realised. Aware that Aubrey was watching him, Vincent glanced up, a sheepish expression on his face.

"Just checking that he's okay," he said gruffly, and dipped his head back into his bowl.

Jeremy reached down and stroked Aubrey and then, shrugging off his coat and dropping the bag of books that he had bought, pulled open the fridge door and peered inside.

Molly looked at him, half-amused.

"Why don't you wait for lunch? It'll only be half an hour or so."

"Because, my dear Molly, I am not starting my diet until the new year. In the meantime, I intend to enjoy myself over the Christmas period. Mostly by eating and drinking and reading. Anyway, what time is Carlos back?"

"Any minute now. He was on breakfasts this morning and his shift at the Lodge should have finished twenty minutes ago. He's got a visitor waiting for him in the garden," she added.

As she spoke the front door rattled and Carlos came through to the kitchen and joined Jeremy at the fridge. Molly moved quickly and nudged them out of the way.

"Lunch will be on the table in a minute."

Carlos grinned and leaned back against the work top.

"You've got a visitor. A girl," she added.

Carlos dropped his shoulders.

"Not Ella? How did she find out where we live?"

Molly smiled.

"She's in the garden."

"Molly, do I…"

"Yes," said Molly firmly. "You do."

She moved over to the window with Jeremy and watched as Carlos walked slowly across the snow covered lawn, head down and hands in pockets, towards the girl with her hood up. She was standing with her back to him and looking up at the sky. Turning, she dropped the hood so that the light snow fell on her pretty face and her dark hair with blue and green strands.

THE END

ALSO BY ALISON O'LEARY

Street Cat Blues (Cat Noir # 1)

Country Cat Blues (Cat Noir # 2)

Beach Cat Blues (Cat Noir # 3)

Summer Cat Blues (Cat Noir # 4)

Sleeping Cat Blues (Cat Noir # 6)

Home Cat Blues (Cat Noir # 7)

ACKNOWLEDGEMENTS

Huge thanks to Sean Coleman and his team at Red Dog Press and also to Bloodhound Books, for bringing the Cat Noir series to life with such enthusiasm. Thanks also to my lovely readers who make it all worthwhile.

In memory also of the lovely Eric Cox, a dear cat who always thought more than he spoke.

ABOUT THE AUTHOR

I was born in London and spent my teenage years in Hertfordshire where I spent large amounts of time reading novels, watching daytime television and avoiding school.

Failing to gain any qualifications in science whatsoever, the dream of being a forensic scientist collided with reality when a careers teacher suggested that I might like to work in a shop. I don't think she meant Harrods.

Later studying law, I decided to teach rather than go into practice and have spent many years teaching mainly criminal law and criminology to young people and adults.

I enjoy reading crime novels, doing crosswords, and drinking wine. Not necessarily in that order.

A NOTE FROM THE PUBLISHER

Thank you for reading this book. If you enjoyed it please do consider leaving a review on Amazon to help others find it too.

We hate typos. All of our books have been rigorously edited and proofread, but sometimes mistakes do slip through. If you have spotted a typo, please do let us know and we can get it amended within hours.

info@bloodhoundbooks.com